MALCHOR THE CONQUEROR

BOOK 1

R.A. MASTERS

Do you want more? Sign Up to receive an email when there's a new release or a sale.

Do you want more? Sign up to receive an email when there's
a new release or a sale.
http://smarturl.it/RAMastersNewsletter

CHAPTER ONE

Everything had been going fine up until I saw her. That blonde-haired beauty, dressed in flowing silk robes--or rather strips of fabric--that did little to cover the most seductively shaped body I'd ever seen. It was hard not to stare in the moment, watching her sun-kissed skin glisten in the midday heat.

She would have been a beauty in any world, but in this hellish landscape? She seemed like a walking mirage. How was I supposed to help myself? I hadn't seen anyone in what must've been months, and then suddenly... her. A big breasted, pouty-lipped damsel in distress.

But first, I should backtrack a bit.

When I say 'everything had been going fine,' I should put a qualifier on that.

If you consider trekking through the wilds alone, surviving off of berries, lizards, carrion birds, and strange, bug-eyed, four-limbed fish to be 'fine,' then I guess you get my perspective.

I realize for most folk that's far from fine. But for me, there was a sort of beauty to it. I'd always craved the outdoors, to get away from civilization, the buzz of technology, the constant demands on my time and attention. Worst of all though was the reality of busting my butt, working in some dreary office or at a computer, just to buy a few more gadgets I didn't much care for.

But I didn't end up in this world on purpose, all the same. Hell, I didn't even know it existed until I was in it. And even then, it took me a while to come to terms with where this place was and what it meant.

I'd always been in search of adventure, you see. Some sign of a fight worth facing, some cause to throw myself into that wasn't just a nine-to-five grind. I loved camping, fishing, hunting, survivalist training, white-water rafting, even cave diving.

It was those last two that landed me in the predicament I was in. Chasing after my next thrill, some challenge to overcome, I'd heard tales of this tunnel in a rapid stream. The Devil's Drop. Half the water of the river vanished down into some hole in the earth, and nobody had ever found out where it led.

Nobody.

I saw my chance to make my mark on the world, to be the first to do *something*.

So I went there one year, and I studied the area. It was big enough for a man to fit down, though with the water of the river pouring in on you, it would've been terrifying even if you knew where it led.

I didn't go down there that first time, though, of course. I crave adventure, but I'm not suicidal. I researched all there was to read up on it, the many failed experiments of dropping floating beacons down the tunnel that eventually vanished without a trace. I studied the charts that mapped it out as deeply as possible. And, most importantly, I surveyed the area, talked to the locals, and gathered information directly.

That was how I came to hear the tales and myths around it. Locals said it was in fact the gateway to Hell itself. Scary stuff for some, right? Well, I didn't give in. I followed up on some clues in the telling, and found out about a nearby cave with some markings. Scientists in the area had apparently heard of it, but dismissed it as an effort by the locals to draw in more tourism money.

Why were they so dismissive? For one, the map carved into the cave wall--at least the upper part of it--too closely resembled the data they'd put together with sonar devices and trackers. They figured there was no way primitive people could've mapped it out so accurately without modern tools. Surely, they thought it must've been just the locals using the scientists' work and guessing how the rest of the tunnel turned out.

Oh yeah... and they might've also doubted it because of some of the pictograms depicting outlandish monsters and beasts down there. None of that could be real, right?

All the same, I took it more seriously. Because I get what the ivory tower intellectuals will never understand: people know the land they live on. You don't work on a swath of land for countless generations without coming to know it intimately. And one intrepid, daredevil explorer armed with only crude rope and his hands is worth more than any device, I say.

So I studied that cave map, and I made use of it.

The next time I came back on a 'vacation,' I was armed with all the best caving equipment: climbing gear, rations, hunting knife, and, of course, a survival machete.

Hey, I didn't believe in monsters either. Machetes have many uses. But also... I wasn't about to get stuck down there without a proper weapon, just in case cave monsters or something else were really down there.

The locals said I was nuts. I agreed. But down I went regardless.

Right away, I started getting second thoughts. Having all that water pour down over me was like being waterboarded as I pulled off some of the trickiest climbing of my life. It felt like dying, truth be told. There are no words terrifying enough to convey how awful it was.

But once I'd begun, I was determined to finish. So down I went.

I was a big guy then. I worked out, ate well, spent all my time in the wilds or practicing wood working. So I was--and am--in great shape. It became a tight fit at times, scarily so with the smooth stone walls pressing in on me from all sides. But those muscles helped save my ass as I slipped on the smooth, slippery stone over and over.

I narrowly avoided cracking my skull open many times. But as I made the last jump across a crevice, my foothold gave way and I had to throw myself further. I cut myself on a jagged stalagmite.

That wasn't even the worst of it. I probably should've turned back there, but I felt on the cusp of something great.

You see, that narrow tunnel had opened up to wider spaces at points, such as where I'd had to leap a crevice. But further down I found the mother of all caverns: a massive, open cave that sprawled on just as far as the eye could see... which, granted, wasn't that far in the darkness. But it matched the cave map the locals had told me about, as far as I could tell, and I saw now that they were right--about the map of the tunnels, at least.

I lowered myself down, dangling from my rope as water poured down beside me into the abyss. I descended to the end of the rope, until I could go no further and see no farther. It was black as the void all around me, with only the sound of that rushing water for company.

But I knew if the cave map was right... the bottom couldn't be much further. It had to be close.

I shone my light down, and could make out a glimmer of smooth rock a few feet below me, close enough that I could make the fall and not be injured. It even looked like I would have been able to jump up and grab my rope again after the fall. So, I did the foolhardiest thing I'd ever done in my life: I let myself drop.

I don't live with regrets, but let me tell you… if I had to do that fall again, I don't know that I'd have the guts for it.

I fell, for what felt like too long, and then I hit hard rock with a thud. I bounced off it, then slid down the shiny rock I'd seen that turned out to be just a small ledge. And over that ledge I went. I had been winded from that first impact and couldn't grab onto anything in time, but as I fell further, I managed to use my climbing pick to try and snag onto the rock wall alongside me.

It scraped the rock but couldn't find a firm hold. The friction slowed me somewhat, but also changed the way I was falling so that my body twisted mid-air, and…

I struck my head against the rock wall. Hard. Real hard. So hard it cracked open the protective helmet I was wearing, ending its service to me.

And even then, the fall wasn't done.

Miraculously, I landed in a pool below with the jolt of the tepid water washing over me, leaving me shocked and disoriented. But there, in that moment as I lay floating facedown in the water, breathless and confused, something caught my eye. There was something glowing in the dark. The faint outline of some object on the bottom of the water.

I rushed to the surface to catch my breath again. Once I sucked in a gasping inhale, I spared little time to appreciate the sight of the cavern walls coated in glowing fungus that hadn't been visible when I had my flashlight on. I took a deep breath and just went right back down for that shiny thing I saw.

When I got to it, I was astonished to find an old necklace, or perhaps a bangle, made with what looked like jade and metal. It was beautiful, but so strange. It didn't match the local style at all, nor anything of the world that I knew, for that matter. At its heart was a jade carving of some horrible, monstrous visage. A face like no other, resembling something out of a horror story.

But I didn't have much time to appreciate it in the moment, so I wrapped it around my wrist for safekeeping. I kicked my way up to the surface to swim around the pool, which soon seemed more like a lake.

It was massive, and it took me a lot of swimming to eventually find some rocks to pull myself up onto. And there I found myself amid a veritable forest... a forest of fungus.

I should've been more concerned for how I would get out, but I was too fascinated. Was I the first man to ever lay eyes on this alien, subterranean world? It thrilled me to think I might be, and I began to wander around, machete in hand. Just in case.

I never saw a monster there, truth be told. But as the fungal 'trees' grew taller than me the further I went, I began to hear things. Like something shuffling around in the dark. Then came a sound like a horrible squeal from some unearthly creature in the distance. And let me tell you, I wasn't about to second-guess the cave drawings this time either.

I ran away from the noise, and that was when I came to it: stairs. Real, honest-to-goodness stone stairs. Part of me was let down that this meant I wasn't the first man to tread here, but then I realized I'd discovered some lost ruins that modern man had never seen before. Just like that, exhilaration filled me again.

Light was scarce I had my flashlight, but it could only shine so far ahead into the ruins. This place was massive. It went on and on. But the more architecture I took in, the less sense it made. It was like nothing I'd ever seen, nothing anyone had ever written about in any story I've ever read, nothing any show or movie had ever portrayed.

I could've lost myself in that place for ages, but that sound of shuffling in the dark grew louder, and another horrible cry filled the air.

So, I ran on into the unknown.

There's nothing I can say to make you understand what it was like, and certainly nothing I can do to understand whatever happened at that point. But the new 'bracelet' I'd acquired seemed to grow icy cold on my wrist, and when I glanced at my wrist in the dark as I ran, I saw it glowing green.

Either by random chance or fate, I found myself in some chamber of a building, where I sought refuge. It was full of terrifying statues and exquisitely hideous carvings on the wall. And at the heart of it loomed a great archway that seemed to respond to the glowing of my new charm.

It was then that whatever was chasing me pounced. I'm telling the truth when I say that I never saw any monster down there, but I did *feel* one. It knocked me over, climbed on my back, and my heart pounded.

I struggled for my life in a brawl with this thing I could not even see.

Luckily, I had my machete, and soon a flow of inky black blood coated me as I hacked at its… neck? I couldn't say, but I'd triumphed. I felt the beast recoil, whether in pain or to recoup for another lunge at me.

What happened next changed everything. That archway seemed to light up at the death of that thing, with freakish runes across its glowing green. And suddenly…

It was like being thrown through space, hurtling faster than the speed of light. My insides very nearly became my outsides, and I vomited upon arrival.

Arrival where? Well… that takes me back to the beautiful blonde.

CHAPTER TWO

I came out the other side into a horrible temple that resembled the one I'd entered at the archway. Except instead of being underground, this temple was perched on the edge of a sun-blasted desert.

At first, I had no idea what to make of it. I tried to rationalize things as best I could, but I concerned myself with survival first and foremost. I needed to find water in this desert, so to speak, and while I had some rations, they wouldn't last forever. So, I needed food, too.

I spent the next few days getting familiar with the environment. Building shelters that were little more than logs and leaves leaned against cliffs, eating whatever I could find that didn't seem poisonous. It wasn't long before the inescapable fact hit me: this wasn't earth. None of the creatures I saw or hunted were like those I recognized. Oh, sometimes they *resembled* creatures of our world. The lizards, for instance, were still lizards, but… not quite like any I knew.

I gambled a few times on what was edible and what wasn't. Had a few bad times, but I got by. Cooking the meat of the lizards and buzzards made it safe to eat, I learned. Berries on the other hand tended to be too risky to try.

When the days turned into weeks, I started to fashion hides to protect myself from the hot rays from above. Snakes and lizards became my new clothes to protect me from the suns.

Yes, suns.

There were two of them, another big tip off that this wasn't earth. I wrote it off as an optical illusion at first, but after a day or so there was no denying it anymore.

With protection from the suns secured, I was able to set off and explore a wider area.

And as weeks grew to months, the thrill of surviving on my own--with only my machete, knives and climbing gear-- took over. I was doing well for myself. Sure, I was alone, but I was living a life that felt… satisfying.

You don't have time to question existence when you're just surviving. And so, surviving brought me peace of mind.

That's when *she* came into my life.

I'd been looking for game to hunt, following some tracks through the sand, when I heard voices. Human voices. The wind carried sounds in strange ways, but I managed to figure out the direction, and my curiosity drove me forward.

At first, I was surprised to see other people, albeit short, haggard-looking people dressed in rags. They were a rough bunch to look at. Some were missing an arm, others an eye. Some just fingers.

I didn't approach them, I just watched from afar…until I saw what they were doing.

Or rather, who they were pursuing.

That beautiful, buxom lass was on her own, running barefoot through the rocky sand up an incline to the ridge above, where I waited.

I was captivated. Not least because those breasts of hers bounced deliciously as she ran.

Now, I know you're probably thinking: really? You're thinking about her tits at a time like this? But to be fair, it was only a moment, and I hadn't seen even a picture of a woman in months. I'm only a man, after all.

And once I pushed away that surprise, I acted as I thought any decent man would. I sprang down with a spear I'd fashioned using a long wooden pole (that wood was damn hard to harvest in a desert, let me tell you) with my knife attached at the end.

Crouching down in a fighting pose, I roared at them to intimidate their band of five.

They froze at once, surprised to see me, and perhaps most alarmed at my size. Like I said, these guys were a hard-looking bunch: scraggly, sporting many wounds fresh and old, as well as lost limbs. Worse, they looked malnourished. That wasn't a surprise if they lived here in this hellish desert.

But after a moment, they regained their fighting spirit and began to advance on me again.

"Out of the way, outlander!" shouted one of them, and I was surprised to see they spoke... English? But I rebounded quickly from that surprise.

"You'll not lay a finger on that girl!" I roared back at them in my booming, most menacing voice. It made them flinch and brandish their own rudimentary weapons.

"That girl is worth a king's bounty! We'll not give her up easily, outlander," snarled the one-eyed man that seemed to lead them. He advanced towards me with a crude spear and shield made of bone or some other stark white material. Perhaps a giant crab shell?

He lunged at me, thrusting forward with his spear. But I dodged it and lashed out with my own, stronger bodied and more prepared. He lifted his shield to block, but whatever material his shield was made of was no match for my stainless-steel knife. It just cut straight through the shield and caught him in the throat under the jaw, ending the man then and there.

The first time I'd ever taken a human life.

I felt a pit in my stomach, but I didn't show it.

"Don't make me kill the rest of you!" I barked as I pulled my spear from the dead man, and watched the others stare in fear. "Get out of here, and leave the girl be!" I shouted at them.

"You don't understand, she's a wanted criminal! The Warlord-King himself wants her!" shouted back one scraggly-bearded man as he brandished a primitive sword in his lone arm.

"I don't care!" I snarled as I jabbed at them.

But desperation must've been driving them hard, because only half of them fled, and the last two charged at me.

I'd been in some brawls before. Whether it was school-yard fights, a drunken bout at the bar, or someone who tried to rob me at gun or knife point, I'd never been the kind of man to lie down and take it. But this was nothing like those times.

These guys were desperate. While I had the advantage of size and strength on them, not to mention a superior weapon, they were tenacious.

They worked together, slashed and jabbing, as I dodged and parried.

But I was the superior fighter, and I wore them down. I plunged my spear through one, then the other, watching blood leak from them, draining more of their energy and spirit. Yet still, they didn't relent. Even after my spear cut down another one of them, the last one kept on, only growling and yelling more ferociously at me as he renewed his assault.

My demands for him to surrender went ignored, and my attempt to give him a chance to do so bought him an opportunity to knock the spear from my hand. Clearly, he wasn't interested in mercy. I'd been disarmed, and he slashed at me with his own sword made of carved, sharpened bone.

But I still had my trusty machete. I drew it off my belt and parried his next attack, knocking the weapon from his hand in the process.

In a moment of stupid panic, he looked back up the slope toward the woman, then tried to dart around me to get to her.

"Stay away from the girl!" I shouted, as I threw out my arm and machete to deter him. But he ran on, and his neck met my blade's edge.

So fell the last of the bunch.

Or, what I thought was the last of them. I didn't even get a moment of relief before I saw a flash of movement out of the corner of my eye. One of the people who fled had somehow returned to get around behind me, and was brandishing his spear as he charged at me...

Only for a pointed blade to come jutting out of his neck with a spurt of blood.

But it was not my weapon.

The blonde didn't flinch from the blood nor the violence, holding the blade in him for a moment, giving it a twist, and then pulling it out. Some of the crimson squirted out from him and onto her partially exposed torso as his heart beat for the last time, and she seemed to find it amusing.

Then she moved toward me, and I've got to be honest, I wasn't sure if I was going to be next. I had underestimated what a damsel in distress could do when given an appropriate distraction for her pursuers.

She licked her ruddy lips as she looked me up and down, and I felt my cock stir, even though I was half terrified of dying. There was something about the way she made me feel so... objectified. Like her emerald gaze was a deep caress, following every glistening muscle up my legs, over my torso, before she finally met my eyes.

"You're a man," she stated, as if that was the most surprising and interesting thing to her, even with several bodies pooling blood at our feet.

I had just saved her (and she had saved me, too, but who's

counting?) but I wasn't a fool. She was clearly comfortable with killing, even if it was just to protect herself. And she had no good reason to assume I wasn't out to cash in on whatever bounty the other guys were after, too. So, she might've come for me next, but all the same…

I don't hurt women. So I lowered my machete, giving it a shake to splatter some of the blood onto the rocks.

"That I am," I said to her, standing tall and straight again, relaxing my battle pose.

I rotated my broad shoulders backward, looming over her just as I had over the other men. Even though she showed no signs of the same malnutrition and brutal living I saw in the men we'd just fought, she was still a woman and therefore not up to my great height. I'd never met a woman who was.

"Are you okay now?" I asked, studying her with what I hoped was a serious expression. In truth, it was hard to hide the fact that every inch of her smooth, toned body was calling to me and making the beast within me stir and roar.

She looked up at me as I stood taller, and she seemed pleased by that in some way I didn't quite understand. I supposed if everyone she met was as bedraggled and broken as the ones who'd been chasing her, I came out looking pretty good by comparison. But there was something else behind her nearly-glowing green eyes that still made the hair on the back of my neck prickle up.

"For now," she said with a seductive lilt to her honeyed voice, "but you must be very new here if you think calm will last any longer than a blink of an eye."

Those words of hers gave me goosebumps. She didn't just *look* like the hottest woman alive, she sounded the part too. Every syllable dripped with seduction. I was surprised she couldn't have handled those men with a simple bat of her long lashes.

"I had months of calm in the desert before coming across you and that… gang," I said to her, looking down at the dead man at my feet. I bent down, wiping my blade clean on his rough-hewn clothes, then stood up and sheathed the machete.

"I am Malcolm, by the way," I said to her, hands on my hips for the introduction.

I was being polite and introducing myself, but I wasn't about to offer her my hand as long as she still had that blade at the ready. I was an imposing figure to her, I assumed. Broad shoulders, barrel chest with rippling abs on display, glistening in the sun. But there was something… different in her eyes.

"Malchor," she said, butchering my name, but making it sound impressive. "I hate to break it to you, but your days of calm in the desert are over now. They know of you, and they'll be coming for you." She reached out with her empty hand, poking my shoulder as if... well, I had no idea what she was doing. It was almost like she was testing to see if I was a mirage. But I had just killed a bunch of guys for her, so if I was a mirage, I was a pretty powerful one.

But, of course, I wasn't a mirage, and her tanned finger pressed into my solid flesh.

"Your months here have not prepared you for what is to come, Malchor. Much worse than they will be pursuing you."

I arched a brow at her in confusion. She was speaking in riddles, and I wasn't sure what her angle was. She wore an obviously expensive silk gown, though it exposed most of her body, the soft fabric caressing her curves. Gold earrings and bangles glinted against her tanned flesh. She looked like some exotic dancing girl out of a movie or story, but there she was in the middle of nowhere, and the only other people seemed to be scraggly, unkempt ruffians.

"I don't know what you're talking about, lady," I said, since I still didn't know her name. But I let her poke and prod at my glistening chest, feeling the hard muscle beneath that had only grown tougher in the months since I got here. I was able to keep eating well, so I never lost any of my bulk, but what little fat I had on me had been stripped away by lots of hard work in the hot sun. "I was just helping a lady in distress, before going back to my business," I said to her.

She laughed at that, and somehow made maliciousness and amusement sound endearing together. Her laugh was almost musical to my ears.

"No, Malchor. You will not be returning to business. You have stepped into something greater than yourself. And to survive it, there are many preparations you need to make. Living off the land is one thing. Thriving off it is something you will only do with help. *My* help," she said, her hand flush against my right pec.

I couldn't help it; I liked the touch of her soft hand on my flesh. I looked down at it, pressed against my hard muscle, then back to her. Though my eyes couldn't help but take in a heap full of her large breasts, which were pushed up by her silken top into thick mounds of cleavage.

"You haven't even told me your name, and I'm supposed to trust that you know what's best for me? C'mon. I'm sure those guys were after you for a reason, even if I wasn't about to let them get you," I said to her, reflecting on how foolhardy I'd been in the first place, jumping between a woman and five angry, armed men.

"Oh baby, you know why those guys were after me," she said, her eyes lidded as she looked up at me. "Wouldn't you chase me to the ends of the world if you were them?"

I was entranced by her, and I had to wonder for a moment if I really wasn't in a strange new world where magic was possible. It felt like she was using sorcery to make me bend to her will.

Of course, she needed no magic to do that. She needed only her supple, perfectly shaped body, her sultry voice, and that soft touch of hers. It stirred my manhood, and put my dick in charge instead of keeping my logical mind in the driver's seat.

"I thought I did," I said at last, my voice lower as I felt the temptation seep into my blood and bones. "But then they mentioned a bounty," I said, my eyes flicking to the bloody dagger in her hand. "You like to carry protection, don't you?"

"There aren't many like me here, and trading in flesh is one of the easier ways to feed and clothe yourself. But I'd rather avoid my flesh being traded without my say-so. Some take issue with that," she said. She smiled in a disarming way, her thumb gently stroking my oiled chest. At my words, she glanced to the dagger, then back to me with a shrug of her perfectly tanned shoulders. "A girl could never be too cautious when finding a strong, handsome man amidst the sea of outcasts."

It all made sense enough for me, at least with the blood draining from my head down to my groin. The fact I'd just been in a harrowing battle didn't help. A good workout or a death-defying encounter always tended to get me good and stiff anyway.

"Then I'm doubly glad I could stop them for you," I said, my hand coming up to grasp her wrist at my chest. I didn't hold it tight or force it away, but I held it nonetheless, letting her feel the strength in my grasp. "Do… you need protection getting somewhere safe? I can do that much for you at least," I offered.

I'd already been overly generous with her, so why I was offering to play bodyguard for a few hours or even a day or two, I don't understand. Actually, I did, because it was those tits I was staring at, those pouty lips, that alluring look from her deep, emerald eyes.

"You can come with me. I was on my way to a place that will be safe for us to rest for a few hours," she said as she took another dainty step toward me. I could feel her chest graze against my abs, and for a moment, she seemed very delicate and needy.

"I have to repay you, after all. But here it's not safe. There will be more of them before the suns meet the sand."

I swallowed, my neck bulging as I tried to push down the feelings that she conjured up in me.

"You don't owe me a thing. I did what I did because I wanted to, not because I expected a reward," I said to her, stubbornly prideful and independent as ever. "But..." I relented, wetting my lips, "I can escort you there, certainly. Especially if more of them are coming."

I stepped back from her, which was a nearly herculean feat of willpower in its own right. Bending down, I picked up the spear that had been knocked from my hands earlier.

She watched me, though her eyes darted back to my machete. I noticed the curiosity in her gaze before she wiped off her own blade and tucked it in a makeshift leather holder strapped to her luscious upper thigh. She was very fit, but she still had that little softness that made the skin indent around the band, and she touched herself there for the briefest of moments. Was she hoping I was watching?

It didn't matter, because a second later, her back was turned to me, the gossamer-like fabric gliding over her ass as she began to lead the way.

What could a man do but follow that luscious ass, no matter the danger it led him into?

CHAPTER THREE

She said the journey wouldn't be but a couple hours, but it turned out to be quite a bit longer. Dusk was approaching as I strode along with her. My gait stretched a lot farther than hers, so the journey was easy, but if her soft figure made me think she lacked endurance, I was wrong. She kept pace without issue, it seemed.

"So," I began, trying to make conversation, "you were an… entertainer, before having to flee for your life?" I asked, choosing my words carefully.

She nodded at me, her blonde hair glistening with the motion.

"Yes, primarily for one man. But when he died, I became somewhat of a coveted prize," she said, glancing over her shoulder at me. She wiggled her ass more noticeably for the next couple of steps for emphasis.

"I can see why," I confessed, not wanting to give her any more leverage over me--or my incessantly throbbing cock--than she already had. But I was unable to deny the truth. "I admire your guts for refusing to take that and going off to make your own way. Not many would dare brave these harsh wilds for any reason… I imagine," I had to tack on.

I knew that to be true in my world, anyway. But perhaps not this one. Maybe these horrid deserts and wastelands were crawling with people I hadn't encountered yet.

"Not many go alone, fewer survive," she agreed. "The only way to make it is to find some like-minded individuals to work with, and protect each other against those..." she trailed off, pausing her words but not her steps. Instead, she started to pick up the pace, pointing at something in the distance.

One of the suns was hanging low in the sky in the direction that she was pointing. The light was gleaming off the sand and distorting everything in the dizzying heat, so it was hard for me to see. But I shielded my eyes, and eventually spotted something dark on the horizon, some sort of black obelisk or pillar.

"We should be able to make it before it's too late, so long as we have some luck!" she said.

I picked up my pace, even though I didn't quite understand her meaning entirely, nor the sense of urgency. My powerful thighs pumped and I kept up with her, spear at my side.

"Too late for what?" I asked, grunting as we ran, watching her flowy silk skirts dance around her long, shapely legs.

"Too late to see the beasts that crawl in the shadows," she said. I imagined she meant nightfall, but didn't know what beasts she was talking about. The closest I could conjure up was the thing I had encountered back on Earth. Before the portal. It seemed like a lifetime ago now.

The thought of its eerie touch, the scaly but smooth hide that had clung to me, clawing at my old vest which had been ripped to shreds in the fight made my skin crawl. I swore I could see writhing figures in the shadows of the cliffside, flitting from rock to rock, as if anxiously awaiting the setting of the final sun.

I picked up my pace at the sight of that, real or imagined.

Sand kicked up around us as suddenly a rumble reverberated beneath our feet.

"What's that?!" I shouted to her.

"The Demon of the Desert awakens!" she said, eyes wide.

"The shadow beasts?" I asked.

"No! Worse than the beasts. Far, far worse!" she said, pumping her long legs faster, her hands slicing through the air as she bolted. In no time she caught back up to my side.

I dared take a look behind us and saw that the trembling of the ground was more intense back there, so much so that sand was cast up into the air in one gritty cloud which seemed to be heading in our direction.

"Fuck," I muttered, and the two of us redoubled our efforts. The looming black obelisk grew closer and turned out to be far larger than I anticipated. It was nestled against the wall of rock behind it, but rising up taller than it, too.

We ran with all we had, and I felt my worn pants strain against my muscular thighs. They had held up remarkably well so far in the desert, but I felt a new tear rip open in the fabric over my thigh from the sheer exertion of the run.

"What the hell is that thing?!" I demanded, daring to glance behind me again and see something on our trail rise up out of the sand. It was a horrible black mound that rose and fell like the waves of the ocean. Except that it was moving through the sandy desert.

"Worry about the 'what' once we get to safety," she called out in a huff, and it was the most frightened I'd seen her so far. Until that point, she had seemed completely unfazed by anything, as if she had everything under her control. I can't deny that her fear panicked me even more, and we both pushed ourselves to the absolute limit. The hot sand was beginning to cool, but that was no relief as each hard footfall displaced more of it, making each step a lot harder than running on open grass or even pavement.

I never thought I'd want to see pavement again in my life,

but at that moment, I wouldn't have minded some asphalt. Hell, concrete would've been a welcome change.

At that point I could feel the presence of the thing behind us, as if it was breathing down my neck. And then… its unearthly roar split the air, reminding me of the thing in the cave, but far bigger and far more grating. If I hadn't been busy pumping my arms to run, I would've had to cover my ears to shield them from the pain of that harsh cry.

But I didn't look back this time. I stayed focused on that obelisk.

Sand picked up in front of us now. The thing was so close, the desert itself was being lifted up in a frenzy around us. I could barely see the obelisk ahead through the darkening sky and the mini sand storm.

"Fuck, fuck, fuck," I cursed under my breath, and then…

It was there in front of me, the smooth marble-like stone stairs rising up. But now the sand was beginning to sink down, as if it was transforming into quicksand beneath our feet.

"Jump!" she cried, and I obeyed, lunging forward toward the promise of safety.

I felt my torso connect with the stone, nearly knocking the wind from my lungs, but I managed to grab onto the edge of the stone, holding it as the sand rushed beneath my feet like a tide rapidly going out.

But my female counterpart was shorter than me, her leap not as long, and only her hands were able to connect with the stone. Her dainty fingers turned white as the sand sank into a pit, her legs thrashing as she fought to pull herself up. She was fighting not only gravity, but a rush of air that sought to fill the void developing around the obelisk, and I grappled my way up, grabbing her wrist.

"Hold on!" I called out, reaching for her other arm and trying to pull her up. I wasn't secured to anything, and now I was fighting her weight along with the intense pressure of the air.

"Don't look at it!" she ordered, and I stared into those wide, green eyes instead. She wasn't telling me to save her, she wasn't telling me to pull her up. She was trying to keep me safe. Warning me of a horror I had no way of being prepared for.

Maybe it was her kindness and compassion that gave me the strength, or maybe it was the way the wind changed, or maybe I was just a lot more badass than even I thought. It didn't matter. All that mattered was the fact that I pulled her up and away from the gaping sand pit and the monster that roared in our ears, helping her onto the smooth, marble-like stone platform.

I grabbed the spear that had fallen from my hands in the jump, and then it was the mysterious woman's turn to take my wrist. She tugged me along, and I saw there was a doorway at the base of the obelisk. In normal times, it might have seemed menacing, the eerie glow that she was leading us to, surrounded by marble. There were carvings on the smooth surface that glimmered in the waning light of day, but I didn't have time to pause to study them. Instead, she dragged me into the sheltered area, and I felt a sense of protection there, enough so that I dared looking back one final time.

My mind ached at the sight of a creature I could only barely glimpse and never truly explain with words. It was the size of a house, at least what I could see of it. It seemed most of it was hidden under the sand as it thrashed and moved in a rage, apparently unable to rise up onto the stone dais to get at us with all its mass, however much there might have been.

I was breathing heavily, and I looked away from that Eldritch abomination. I felt a hole in the back of my mind, where my memory tried to cling to the sight of it. But it was better left forgotten.

I headed inside, where light was spilling down from the setting suns, amplified by mirrors, I presumed, to cast its rays over the room. It was adorned with great statues of animal-headed women in various states of undress or displays of sensuality.

It seemed vacant, or at least there were no signs of life that I could see, and we took a moment to catch our breaths. I was bent over, my hands on my thick thighs, my chest heaving, so I didn't notice how close she'd gotten to me. I looked up, and there were her tits right in front of me exposed from her dress that must have gotten torn open on the sharp stone.

I started to avert my eyes, to be a gentleman, but then her lips were on mine, electric and soft. We had just escaped a fate worse than death, I knew that much, but the intensity of her kiss made me wonder if it was somehow even more terrifying than that. It was as if she was vibrating with sensual energy, and she was trying to pour it into me through the meeting of our mouths.

Had I still held full control of my wits, I might've broken away from the kiss then and there. She was a stranger, and one I knew could kill without batting an eye when the moment called for it. But after two death-defying moments in one day, and the sight of her stunningly flawless body taunting me the whole time…

I accepted it. I melted into those pouty lips of hers, kissing her back as I let my spear rest on the floor and simply gave in.

My two hands came up to her hips, my palms so big and rough on her smooth flesh, sliding back to just above her thick bubble of a rear as we made out, our lips smacking in the eerily lit hall.

I hadn't been with a woman in so damn long, and never with one so stunning as her. My manhood was raging in my tattered pants, so I accepted the kiss, dove into it greedily, and squeezed her supple body with a groan of desire.

She clung to me, her skin still hot from the sun and slick

from the run, so that she glided against me as she lifted herself up onto me. Her thick, sumptuous thighs wrapped around my hips, and I felt the heat of her sex so alluringly close to my cock. I felt her dagger still strapped to her leg, but her arms were tight around my neck, so I didn't need to worry about that right then.

She seemed to want me as much as I wanted her. I still didn't know her name, but that seemed pretty unimportant when she started grinding against my lower abs. Her teeth found my lower lip, biting me gently, teasing me with her tongue.

If I said that part of me wanted to break it off and question her about why she was doing this, to see if she was giving into the same passionate urges that stirred in me, or whether this whole thing was out of some sense of obligation, to repay a debt, I'd be lying.

It was hard to resist the way her hips moved and the heat of her loins. She felt as fiery and primed for this as I was. I just let my strong hands slide back to her ass, cupping those bare, supple cheeks through the slits in her skirt, sinking my grip into those two smooth curves as my cock throbbed with incessant need.

"Who are you?" I asked, my voice hazy and drunk with lust.

She didn't answer. Instead, her mouth went to my neck, kissing and licking me, tasting that clean sweat off my skin. Her back arched, pushing her ass into my hands, her huge tits rubbing against my chest. I hadn't had time to appreciate it in the short glance I got, but I felt her nipples harden against me, adorned with metal that made them even stiffer.

"Take me to the dais," she said, and I had no idea what she was talking about. But then she gestured, and I saw some sort of stone platform at the other end of the room where the mirrors seemed to coalesce. The suns had set and now the light was of a clearer blue tinge glowing from the large moon that loomed overhead. It was twice the size of the moon on Earth, which was lucky, as it shed more light when it was at its fullest peak, like it was that night.

I couldn't help but oblige her.

Back in my old life, I never could tolerate orders. Not from anyone. I'd tried a stint in the military because I wanted the skills it offered and I wanted to do something that mattered. But I found it was just more orders being barked at me by petty jerks and fighting battles that mattered to nobody I could see, so I didn't sign up for a second tour. Back in civilian life, I didn't fare much better. I am too headstrong to be obedient.

But when this stunningly hot woman told me to take her to the stone slab, I felt compelled to do it. I carried her over, and planted her backside down upon it as she pawed and kissed at me. My cock was straining to burst out of my trousers; after all, I wasn't thinking with my clearest head. I kept grinding my dick up against her as I fondled her soft flesh, letting my hands roam up her sides to cup her ample breasts, feeling them and their piercings, surprised at how heavy those perfect tits were.

She reached down between her thighs, and the soft silk panties she wore were quickly torn away and tossed behind her. This let the scent of her sex flood my nostrils, and the way she parted her legs, digging her heels into the table and lifting her hips up was deliciously obscene.

It would have been too outlandish even for most of the porn I've seen to see a hot woman presenting herself to a man so desperately. Her pussy lips glistened in the moonlight, her emerald eyes nearly glowing as they stared at me, waiting for me to accept her offering.

"Malchor," she purred, her fingers going between her legs, parting her thighs wider for me. It was so lewd, so brazen, yet so fascinating. She was so beautiful and perfect, and so damn horny. For *me*!

I was beyond caring about how she took my name and transformed it into something alien. The name that probably made sense to her ears, but was strange to mine. All the same, I was entranced by the sight of her body, presented on offer like that. Her heavy tits jiggled as she shifted back, her glistening pussy so slick and ready.

There was no doubt she wanted it. No doubt that it wasn't just some obligation. A woman doesn't get wet like that when she's just returning a favor.

So instead of moralizing or quibbling about it, I just began to undo my belt and peel my trousers off. I added the aroma of my cock's heady musk to the mix of scents in the air as my thick shaft spilled out, hard and more than ready. I grasped her ankles as I positioned myself over her.

She was so fit, so flexible, and she seemed more than comfortable to let me take control of her body. To let me pull her ankles up, resting them against my shoulders as she continued to play with her pussy for my delight.

If I'd gotten my rocks off in the last day or so, I could've watched the show for longer, taken more time to appreciate how her hand went up to that jeweled piece around her nipple and tugged on it a little before letting her fingers smooth over her firm tit. Her dress was in tatters around her torso, her skirt now just pieces of fabric that gathered around her waist, and she offered herself up to me.

Bare.

Fuck, I'd never actually had a girl raw before, as a rule. I never wanted to be tied down to anyone and always took precautions, even if she said she was on the pill. Before I fell into this strange new world, I would've thought more about it. About how I didn't want to risk knocking up a woman I'd just met, no matter how hot and willing she was.

But this was a new world, and a man doesn't turn down a once-in-a-lifetime opportunity to bareback a fantasy girl at a time like this.

At that moment, I just lined up my cock with her tiny little slit, pressed it into those flowering petals and teased her. Or, well, I'd like to say I was teasing her, but mostly it was just the fact that her pussy was so tight and tiny, and I was using my hands on her ankles, that caused me to glide my veiny shaft up over her clit a few times in the process.

I finally got it right, and started to stretch those puffy labia around my dick. I moaned so deeply, the loud, rumbling sound filling the halls as I slid into the tightest, wettest, most perfect little pussy I could've ever imagined. No previous hookup could compare to the fiery hot grasp of her cunt.

"My fires burn for you, Malchor," she moaned, and yeah, I knew that already. She was molten hot around me, and the deeper in I pushes, the hotter her core felt. I don't know if it was the condoms or what, but I couldn't recall another woman feeling like this, so turned on, so absolutely desperate for my dick. So hot, physically and metaphorically.

It was a perfect sight, and as her fingers moved back away from her pussy lips, I caught sight of another piece of jewelry, this one through the hood of her clit. A little red gem was embedded in the gold, and as her clit swelled up, I could see the pressure on it start to grow.

"Fucking gorgeous," I muttered, holding myself there, several inches of my dick still exposed as I throbbed within her tight grip.

I was in awe of this woman who was all fire and sensuality. She was the embodiment of feminine sexuality. And with our difference in size, my dick was like a massive totem, stretching out her pretty little pink lips until they were nearly red from strain. It was beautiful, beyond beautiful, let me tell you.

I didn't waste time. Instinct and desire took over as I grabbed her and moved my hips back. The tight sleeve of her pussy clenched around my dick as I pulled back, causing us both to moan, only for me to shove it back into her with a strong thrust, grunting and shivering with the sensations as I did.

Even then I knew it was a fuck I would never, ever forget. The feeling of our raw loins rubbing, grinding, throbbing together. I savored it as I moaned and spurted precum into her.

She closed her eyes and arched her back as I thrusted into her so deeply, down to her very core. I felt her shudder with pleasure. Her pussy almost seemed to vibrate around my cock, clinging to me so perfectly. Each thrust sent her bouncy tits jiggling, the decorative jewels that stiffened each nipple glittering in the moonlight streaming through the hall.

She was moaning muttering something that I couldn't understand. I guessed that English wasn't her original language and that she was just cursing in her mother tongue, because those sweet gasps were peppered with 'ohs' and 'ahs', and every once in a while, she'd even moan my name.

Well, she'd say *Malchor*. Close enough.

Seeing her writhe beneath me, feeling her pussy tight and wet around my dick, I didn't give a shit about the unearthly horror that was still outside. The place she'd led us to seemed unreachable, wherever it was, and honestly...

If I had died in that moment, I'd have died a very happy man.

But luckily, that monster wouldn't get a chance to face the likes of me, because the thought of cumming in a woman bareback suddenly had an *intense* appeal to me. A much stronger urge than the call to fight. Back on Earth, unprotected sex was not my thing. I would not have dreamed of it. But with every thrust into this mystery woman, my desire to fill her with my seed grew. It was quickly becoming all-consuming.

I know you're probably judging me now. Fucking a woman I'd just met, bareback, telling you about how damn badly I wanted to blow my load in her and knock her up.

What the hell was wrong with me, you ask? Well, let me tell you: if you could see her body, feel the way she wrapped around your dick, you'd have done no different. No man with a hint of heterosexuality in him could have resisted any better than I did in that moment.

My cock was guiding the way now, throbbing incessantly inside her, stretching her little pussy even wider. My thrusts were becoming faster, harder. The sound of our slick bodies slapping together wetly echoed throughout the room, and the tight clench of her cunt was all I could focus on, all I could feel anymore. Whenever I pulled my hips back, it felt as though she was trying to tug me back inside of her. And whenever I pounded in, her cunt rewarded me with the most satisfying squeeze imaginable.

I'll admit now: it wasn't my longest bout of sex. It was no marathon session, but considering what she had to offer, I'll say: no man stood a chance of lasting more than a couple seconds inside her anyhow. Not with all those sensations, not with the way she looked at me, the way her dainty hand toyed with her tits, or the way her other hand reached out to caress my hard pecs and abs.

"Fuck...! I'm gonna… gonna…!" I couldn't get it all out. Words were getting nearly impossible to form.

"*Malchor*," she screamed, and the room went dark.

I know you think I mean that figuratively, especially because at that moment, I came the hardest I've ever come in my life. It wouldn't have been a huge surprise if I had temporarily blacked out from overwhelming pleasure. But as soon as she said my name, the room *literally* went dark. Seconds later, I heard the shattering of the mirrors all around us, collapsing in on themselves with miniscule shards of glass everywhere.

And all I could do was thrust into her as deeply as I could, intent on sowing my seed in her fertile depths, as more foreign words spilled from her lips.

There was no tearing away my focus from her now, even as glass shattered all around us and the room went dark, then lit up again with a faint, eerie glow, enough to catch glimpses of her stunningly beautiful body, glistening in the dark.

I jerked my hips and thrusted my dick into her as far as it would reach as thick strands of my seed shot off into her depths. My eyes rolled back into my head and closed while I grasped her voluptuous body tightly in my arms, and savored the exquisite sensations. The moment that my cum flooded her, filled her, sowed itself inside her as I bellowed like a lion's roar.

I was lost--lost to this world and to that one. I couldn't think, couldn't do anything except enjoy every throb of my dick as it spurted out days' worth of backed-up seed.

I lifted her hips up higher, leaned over her so that her knees were pressed to her torso, pinning her there. I was operating on instinct by that point, wanting my come to take purchase in her. I didn't want to waste a drop, and so I held her there for a long time, our bodies pressed together. She was flexible enough for me to lean in and kiss her, and she kissed me back with such tenderness and love it almost surprised me.

Then she whispered to me, "Touch my clit. Make me cum on you. Then my womb will flower."

You might think that, after emptying my balls, some sense would have returned to me., that my rational brain might've gotten back in the driver's seat and told me, 'wait, *I don't want this babe knocked up with my kid and in need of me to look after them for years on end.'*

But something had come over me, something deeper than just the desire itself. I slid my hand up to her waist, my thumb moving in to tease and press upon her clit. And even though I'd just come, I began to pump my hips again, my dick rock hard and showing no sign of softening as I gave her what she asked for and more.

"Take it," I growled, and it felt as if my cock had swollen and expanded, my balls heavier, as I lustily claimed her atop that slab.

The tiny jewel pressed into my thumb, and I quickly figured out how to use it to make her breath quicken and her pussy squeeze around me. Her mound was positioned straight up, and even the tight convulsing of her pussy didn't spill any of my seed. It didn't take long before she was babbling nonsense, moans peppered with my name.

And then a scream split the air. I felt a jolt go through her body, into me, and back again. It wasn't like anything I had ever experienced before. It was a connection with another person on a primal level, as if we really had just become one, for a brief moment in time.

Her pussy gushed around me, milking my recently-spent cock and daring me to unload again.

Now, in case you think I'm bragging and bullshitting you about my prowess, let me be clear: I haven't been able to fuck back-to-back and cum twice in a row like that in years.

But suddenly, I knew it deep inside: that I could and would go again. I pounded down into her harder. Our toned, fit bodies moved in perfect unison as I hammered inside of her, grasping her body while I fucked her with raw intensity. I swear, that place quaked with my roar of satisfaction.

I made her scream and moan and scream some more, and I was roaring my lust right there with her. Soon, I felt the need to cum again, that fiery trail of virile seed beginning to travel up my shaft, ready to unload once more.

"Malchor the Virile! Malchor the Just!" she squealed, and her pussy walls tightened around me, gripping me and milking me of my second seed.

It was even more intense than the first, sensations I'd never felt before coursing through my entire body. I'd never felt so powerful, so in control as right then, at my most uncontrolled, intent on knocking up this perfect stranger.

She was cumming again, our bodies working in unison to push every ounce of my seed into her womb and shamelessly bind our fates forever together.

I had changed, something had been *done* to me, and in that moment, I knew I'd never be the same again. While Malcolm would've resented that, Malchor wasn't capable of regretting it. Some raw core of masculinity in me had been unleashed, in a way I had never known possible.

I held and groped that beautiful woman. I fucked her raw and hard. I blew my load into her twice, and kept grinding and fondling her as the last of it spilled. I bent down and kissed her breasts, then suckled that pierced nipple as we lay atop the stone slab, basking in the afterglow of our intense climaxes.

No, I'd never be the same. And it was all because of her, that damned place, and the muttered incantations I mistook for babbles of pleasure. There was no time to dwell on it, though, because things were about to get a lot more interesting, *fast*.

CHAPTER FOUR

I had just fucked the most stunning woman I'd ever seen, blown my load in her twice, and still I felt like I could go again. Something in me had changed, but not enough to make me put aside everything that had happened.

So, as I loomed over her, my broad chest heaving, I looked her in the eyes with an intense stare.

"What did you do to me?!" I growled, in a voice that seemed to have more force to it than ever before.

But even if she'd been willing to play ball and answer me, there was no time. Because all around us the sickening sound of cracking stone filled the air.

I had to look away from her to peer around the dimly-lit chamber. And what I saw defied all reason.

The statues of women, with beautiful human bodies but the heads of animals, were coming to life. They were breaking from their pedestals, moving in a strange fashion that I might've called robotic except... it wasn't quite that either. They moved like humans, but not at all. It was clear they weren't truly alive.

"What the fuck is happening?!" I demanded, pulling out

of that nameless, entrancing woman and grabbing for my weapons.

"Fuck," she cursed, cupping her sex as I unceremoniously left her pussy drooling my cum. She shimmied off the dais, but didn't reach for her weapon. Instead, she went to one of the shattered mirrors, finding one of the larger pieces and holding it up like a shield.

"We need to get out of here," she said over her shoulder. "Your spear won't help with these. Perhaps that other weapon you have may, but..."

We didn't have a lot of time to ponder the issue, because the stone-women were advancing on us. And while their bodies were stone replicas of beauty, the menacing visages of animal heads approaching us was far from alluring.

"Where do we go, then?" I demanded to know, but out of the corner of my eye I glimpsed something: a hidden door behind the largest statue, that of a giant woman wearing very little. Her ensemble might've been described as bondage gear back home, but there, it fit in with the aesthetic of the temple. She looked like some goddess of BDSM all the same to me, frankly.

"There!" I bellowed, pointing to the door as one of the statues moved within range of me, and--with a speed that surprised me--lashed out with long claws. I only barely managed to avoid the blow, but my dodge backward put me within range of another menacing stone-woman.

This time, I jumped up onto the stone slab we'd just fucked upon, as my nameless companion ran for the back exit. I watched as stone claws raked over the marble I stood on, rending five furrows into the solid rock.

"Fuck," I said, kicking at the head of the statue. My foot connected with the statue, but it had to have hurt me more than it. I felt a jarring pain shoot up my leg and spine. But all the same, it did set the statue-woman off balance, and she teetered backward.

"Come on!" cried my companion, waving for me to follow. But I had to buy a bit more time. I turned my machete around, not wanting to blunt the sharp side, and attempted to parry another claw attack from one of the statues.

I struck hard stone, and saw cracks fissure up the thing's arm. I repeated my strike, and sent almost half her arm falling to the floor. But again, the jarring blow shot up my arm, too. It would be too hard to take them all down like this; I'd be feeling the aches for weeks, even if I won. And I had a feeling even my steel machete wouldn't last long enough to get the job done.

So I turned and jumped down, following after my companion as I dodged more slashes from the statues' claws.

But then I saw something even more alarming: the giant statue of that goddess was coming to life, as well. It was several stories tall, and would barely be able to move around in the enclosed hall, but realistically, it wouldn't need to.

"Shit," I swore.

My companion watched me, saw the giantess begin to awaken, and she lifted her portion of the mirror. Seconds ticked by as the grinding and lurching of stone filled the room until, finally, the piece of mirror caught the moon's light, and she began to direct it toward the stone statue's face. There was a maddening cry, something that I felt more than heard as it reverberated through my bones, and the largest statue recoiled from the light.

Even though it seemed to do nothing more than disorient the giantess statue, it was a distraction, and thus bought me time. So, as I parried a strike from a statue, then dodged another, I ran ahead, right toward the giant goddess screeching in a pained rage.

My life had gotten crazy in short order, but I never imagined I'd be charging full-tilt at a giant living statue of some sex goddess.

But just as I was almost there, the reflective light of the

mirror seemed to lose its potency. And the colossus saw me. She bent down in her slow, lumbering way to make a grab for me, and I had to jump and slide away to avoid her clawed grasp. I slid between her two giant feet, then watched as she lifted one up to stomp on me, like I was just some bug.

"Fuck!" I cursed again, rolling away and narrowly avoiding becoming toe-jam for a colossus.

But the problem was that even as big and slow as she seemed, she moved surprisingly quickly. She kicked at me as I was getting up. I had to throw myself forward, not a jump, but a tumble. I hit the stone with a thud that left me winded, and it slowed my reaction time for the next move. So, even though I was close to the door now, I was delayed for a precious, vital moment as I tried to get back up.

I could feel the looming presence of that giant statue behind me, ready to strike again, and I knew my timing wouldn't be up to it. But then came my companion's hand, grasping my wrist and pulling me forward.

She was much smaller than me, and had no way to lift or drag my larger body. But that extra help still made all the difference, and I narrowly evaded having every bone in my body crushed as we ran through the small back door that was far too tiny for any of the statue-women to fit through.

"We gotta get out of here. There'll be more guardians," she said, and even in that moment of panic, she still looked radiant. Her dress was almost completely torn to shreds, the strips of fabric exposing much of her thick thighs, her tits bared to me with her stiffened nipples...

I couldn't let myself get distracted, but her soft, plush lips and her wide, vibrant eyes were magnetic.

"We'll need to find a cave. There are rumors of entire towns being forged into the cliffsides, somewhere in this region. But we have to walk carefully to not draw the attention of the Elder Beast. We need to walk like something inhuman. Lurching, hopping, uneven. Vary your stride. The moon is full and will guide our way."

I nodded as we ran along, and peered back to see the temple guardians hammering at the doorway, beating at the stone to make it wider.

"Fine. But you still owe me answers," I growled at her as we raced down the tunnel, past branching paths, not entirely sure where we were going but knowing we had to keep moving.

Finally we reached a fork in the path, where heading straight was no longer an option. My companion paused for just a moment and said, "This way!"

We took one side, and ran past what appeared to be multiple crypts or ritual chambers. Relief washed over me as we caught a glimpse of moonlight in the distance.

When finally we broke out to the other side, we were bathed in that silver moonlight, looking out over a new stretch of desert. Although, this patch was different from the last, somehow. There were more outcroppings of rock in the sea of sand, and it looked newer and less worn than the desert we'd passed.

But we still had to climb down the side of the cliffs from the temple exit. And almost right away, we were assaulted by some of those shadowy beasts. But these I could handle. I reared back and struck fiercely at one that leaped toward me, slicing it in half with my blade.

Another quickly came at me, though. I couldn't get my machete up in time and had to kick it away. It turned out to be a longer fight than I hoped for, as I fended off one, gutted another and then...

I saw my companion--that tricksy witch--being swarmed by them. And though I had plenty of reason to be upset with her, both for her lack of answers and her strange meddling with my mind, in that moment I felt only rage. Rage that someone--*something*--would dare touch what was mine. I let loose a mighty roar as I stabbed through one of the creatures, then went for her.

I barreled toward her like a raging bull, and while she'd done an admirable job on her own, having sliced one open and cut another, she was overwhelmed by the throngs of creatures.

That was my time to shine. I dashed in to jab my spear through one atop her, then swung the machete to slice off the head of another.

I had never used both of those weapons at once before, but suddenly I felt like I had the strength and prowess to do it. To do *anything*. I was a raging terror as I tore through the ghastly things, until the last one was gone.

Their inky black blood splattered all over me, but I didn't relent. And as I saw some more of them coming to join in, I didn't wait. I attacked them head-on with a terrible fury. I was oblivious to the fact that I was now pantless and mostly nude. I was all rage and righteous anger as I shredded those beasts. Then I watched as more of them turned and ran in fear, until it was just me, surrounded by their corpses.

My chest heaved as I caught my breath, and I turned, putting my machete back in its sheath before reaching down to pick my woman up.

The look on her face...

I'd never forget it.

It was intoxicating, and I could never do justice to put it into words, but I knew how that look made me feel. Like I was a king, someone to be admired and feared, worshiped and adored, praised for the rest of my days.

I didn't stop to question the fact that she wasn't surprised by my heroics. It was like she'd known all along that I'd be able to take down those hordes, but she was still in awe of my prowess just the same.

"Thank you," she said. She dipped her head demurely, making my ego swell even more.

I had felt so many emotions in so little time: fiery, passionate emotions. While of course I knew what lust, anger and pride had felt like back in my old life, they were but pale imitations of what I felt in that moment.

What was lust for some picture of a hot woman on the internet compared to a real beauty right in front of me in the flesh, worshipfully ready to meet my needs?

Anger? Yes, I knew that one well. Anger at shitty bosses, anger at how I didn't fit in the world, anger at how there was no place for someone like me in it. But those were hollow emotions, rage without a purpose. It was no comparison to the righteous anger that came from defending what was mine, and being able to fight for it.

As for pride? I'd been proud of things I'd built. Like my cabin, or some equipment I'd made. But the pride of victory, of knowing I was the champion over men and beasts alike in a do-or-die combat, of having a fiercely beautiful woman that was mine, all mine, who looked to me like I was King? There was no comparison.

"Let's go," I said to her, now that I'd hauled her up and set her back on her feet. But I no longer felt the same sense of urgency as we made our way down the cliffs, knowing that these beasts were my bitch now. When push came to shove, I not only beat them, I made them scurry away in fear.

My female companion obediently followed after me, my cum still staining her thighs and marking her as mine as she climbed down along with me.

I knew I had changed back there, that she had done something to me. But it seemed to change her, as well. It was hard to put my finger on what it was, but she just seemed a little softer. Maybe she was just responding to the changes she saw in me.

Either way, it didn't matter the what or the why. All that mattered was that I was going to get us to safety.

We had no trouble from the shadow beasts the rest of the

way down. Well, I should clarify: we had no trouble worth mentioning. A few did try to nip at us, but I ended them quickly and easily, which served as a helpful reminder to the rest to fuck off and leave us alone.

But once we hit the sand, my beautiful woman turned to warn me again about how we had to move to avoid the wrath of the Desert Demon.

Whether we were exceptional at avoiding it, or perhaps it was just slumbering, we didn't feel the sand stir beneath us as we made our way toward the rocky outcrop. Nights seemed to last longer here, though I had no real way of comparing to nights on Earth. It just felt like time moved differently, but my watch had stopped working once I stepped through the portal, so it was difficult to analyze.

My companion was quiet on our journey, though she stayed close to my side, just a step or two behind. She was letting me lead the way, and told me as much in those subtle ways of hers I was starting to learn. The swish of her hips, the way she averted her eyes in deference. I was becoming more able to read her moods pretty well, I thought, but she was still an enigma wrapped up in a perfect body.

At last, we found a cave amid the rocky outcroppings in the sea of sand. We entered it, weary and tired. She showed me how to use the sand to wash away some of the blood and grime we'd accumulated, and we settled into the cool, but comfortable spot.

Yeah. After all we'd been through, a rocky cave did actually feel comfortable.

"Tell me your name," I commanded her. My voice was rough and deep as I looked down at her, unashamed of my relative nudity.

She lay back on the stone, her heavy breasts parting slightly, her hand resting on her stomach as she looked up at me.

"Aphaera," she said, the soft syllables rolling off her

tongue. It was pure femininity, and contrasted so well with the harsher name of Malchor that she'd given me.

"What was that place back there?" I asked her next, giving no sign of how much I still desired her as she lay there looking delicious enough to eat.

"A temple of worship for a great and terrible Goddess," she answered, looking at me intently. It seemed like she was finally willing to give me some idea of what was going on, at least.

I took a moment to think about it as I peered out the cave entrance. Nothing bothered us, and the shadow beasts seemed too afraid to cross the sands themselves. So, I could rest assured that our little island in the sea of sand was protected from their late-night visits, at least.

"So we've pissed off a great and terrible Goddess," I remarked, looking back to her. "What was it you did back there?" I asked.

"We didn't piss off the Goddess, just the guardians of that temple," she said, as if that made it all better. "Well, she *might* be pissed, but it was all done in her name. We just didn't go through the proper channels," Aphaera said as she rolled onto her side, her soft curves illuminated by the sliver of moonlight.

"What we did was unlock your potential. I promised I would help you survive, and I did just that and more. Now, you will thrive, Malchor. We should have waited for the Priestess' blessing. But I didn't want to wait."

I could feel the truth in her words and l the new confidence and virility in me that she'd awoken. But still, I balked at being led along and having my fate messed with by another being. Even if she was a beauty beyond imagining, a beauty that was now mine.

So I stepped toward her, looming large and threatening. But I reached down and brushed some of her wheat-blonde hair out of her face with my mighty hand.

"I don't tolerate being toyed with," I said to her in a low, firm voice. "I've wanted to rip the heads off of men for far less," I said. I thought of the time a former boss messed with my schedule just to throw his weight around and how I had to put the fear of god into him after work to set things straight.

"And now you won't have to tolerate it," she said, her head pushing toward my hand like that of an affectionate kitten. "There is more power in these lands, beyond your knowing, but you hold the key to unlocking it. I will help you," she purred, those emerald eyes locking with mine. "I will swear myself to be bound to you in your journey."

Again, I felt the truth in her words. As though this world was laid open as a playground for me to enjoy, to conquer, to rise above. Like it was less of a perilously harsh realm, and more like some kind of video game for me to beat and reign over. It was just up to me whether I wanted to take on the challenge.

"What do you want?" I asked at last. I stroked her cheek and felt her soft skin under my palm and fingertips. My other hand reached out to caress her breast, then enjoy a squeeze, treating her as mine and helping myself to her body.

"To see you rise up," she grinned, lasciviousness in her tone, "and mold this world into something new. Something worthy of you."

She let me touch her, explore her body, and I knew it was exciting her as well. Even though I'd just fucked her a few hours ago, she was still writhing on the floor at my feet. Ready for me.

"And to carry my child," I said to her with my hand drifting down to her stomach. I caressed that taut, toned belly, imagining it swelling up with my seed. "Or at least that's what you seemed to be excited for a few hours ago," I remarked, licking my lips as I eyed her.

I felt like more of a man than ever, but with that feeling

came my response to her femininity. To resist a beautiful, will-ing, fertile woman now seemed alien to me. As a true man, worthy of her adoration and respect, I was also insatiable. Hungry for her feminine flesh.

"It would be my greatest pleasure," she agreed, her hand resting on top of mine on her stomach. "You will spawn many great children who will support you. But I want to carry the first." She stared at me with such hunger and intensity in her gaze. "The Goddess will bless us, for it is her way. She enjoys a little chaos from her devotees."

I studied Aphaera, her beauty, her willing body. I scruti-nized her for some sign of a lie or deception. I could see none, but she was a cunning woman. I knew I couldn't count out the idea of her playing me, using me.

"I never wanted children back in my world," I confessed to her.

My sudden confession seemed to come out of nowhere. Back in my old life, I was never one to spill the beans, to divulge my desires, my secrets. I kept a cool front, a stony exterior. I never revealed anything valuable about myself if I could help it.

"It never seemed like a place fit for people to live in. So cold, so distant. So full of people who didn't care about anything but more money, more trinkets. No way of winning, just an endless game of scrambling for more money, just for the sake of having it."

"There are some like that in this world. But it is not filled with their kind. And when you take the power of this land, it will be you who molds it to your liking," she said, leaning in toward me and licking her lips like a hungry lioness. "I will care for you and our son, and you will find a bounty of warmth and companionship laid out for you."

I stared into her emerald eyes that seemed to have such a strange glow to them. She was like some ethereal being, too beautiful to be real. And yet, she was.

Then her words hit me.

"Son?" I asked, brow raised, as I swept my eyes over her. "How can you know that? Or even that we will have children? We just fucked; who knows if it even took?" I pointed out.

"It will always take for you now," she said. She leaned up and began to crawl up my legs, her dainty hands caressing my thighs. "You will breed an army," she promised, kissing my abs, teasing me with her tongue. "With or without the Priestess' permission, the Goddess granted you that power."

I stared at her, watching her move in to kiss and paw at me with such reverence. I sat back and let her do it for the time being, pondering it all.

"Every time?" I asked dubiously, brow raised. "And I never agreed to settle down with you. You're beautiful--hot as fuck, in fact--but I only said I'd escort you to safety, not take on the obligation of protecting you forever and raising a family… or an army together," I said with a huff.

She tilted her head, looking up at me with some confusion.

"I cannot birth you an army, Malchor, as much as I wish I could. Just the first of many, your commander." Her fingers crawled up my thighs, moving closer until she was near enough that her bare breasts pressed against my hard cock.

"If you leave at dawn, you will still be great. But with me at your side you will be unstoppable. The choice is yours."

The sight of her bare breasts, pierced with those jewels, pressing up against my exposed hard cock would leave an imprint on any mind. But I was struggling to maintain control here, to keep in command of not only the situation but my own desires. I worked over her words in my mind.

"Wait," I said, licking my lips, "if you're saying you're not going to bear all my children, then who else is going to?" I asked, my cock throbbing at the idea.

"Any you choose worthy of your seed," she said, her

mouth moving along my abs. "I know of some who would make powerful concubines for you, should you choose to keep me as your Chief Consort."

I could tell she thought it would be a special thing, to be my 'Chief Consort', whatever the fuck that was.

"Chief Consort?" I repeated, the term completely unfamiliar to me.

"Main concubine. The head of your harem," she explained.

Main concubine.

I never even settled into a long-term relationship back home, and here this beautiful woman was trying to talk me into maintaining a whole harem of women to be at my beck and call. I have to admit, it was tantalizing. My cock certainly liked the idea, as it throbbed and twitched between her massive tits.

"So, you're saying that you'll bear my children, service my needs obediently, and help me find other women to fuck and knock up?" I asked in disbelief as I looked into her emerald eyes. "All for what? To someday breed an army and…?"

She looked up at me, one of her hands reaching toward my cock. She held it firmly in her grasp as she began stroking my enormous length.

"I want you to give me purpose, Malchor. To help you forge something new, and bring ruin to the evil men who are touched by demons and madness. In you, I see hope. Is it so strange that it would be you, with your legendary weapons and battle-hardened body and knowledge of the things beyond the stars that would be sent to save us? To save me?"

"Purpose," I repeated, staring down at her with heavily-lidded eyes. I was unable to tear my gaze away from those perfect tits, that dainty hand wrapped around my cock, pumping it with such an expert grasp. I really should have stopped her from touching me, so I'd have a chance of keeping a clear head as we talked.

But I hadn't stopped her. I had let this irresistible woman lead the way again, this time in conversation. And worse yet, her words spoke to me in a way I never expected.

"I had no purpose back in my world," I said with a sigh as she worked my cock, which somehow seemed even bigger and bulkier than before. "I was a fighter with no battle worthy of being fought. All the wars of value were over. No room for a man to fight against what was wrong anymore. I could accept it as it was, or struggle to rouse people to the battle cry... but they would never hear it. Because they had distractions, things to keep them busy, glowing screens putting a spell over them to keep them blind to how wrong everything around them truly was," I said, babbling my innermost thoughts to this vixen.

She seemed fascinated, perplexed.

Saddened.

"A man like you should be heard. *Will* be heard. I will teach you about your enemies, of those with power who abuse it. I will keep you abreast of the worthy battles being fought, and the struggles that people will eagerly rally against. Your words will be told in stories for generations to come," she purred seductively, stroking my cock faster as her own excitement rose. "Your likeness will be carved into great stones, and women will flock to you, pleading for your gift. But your power must be wielded wisely, and you must know your enemies well so that you don't plant your seed in their fields."

The way she worked my manhood was masterful. I'd paid for sex back in the real world--a man's gotta try everything at least once--and as amazingly skilled as she was, she had nothing on Aphaera.

I sighed as she coaxed some more pre-cum out to coat the tip of my manhood and spurt a little onto her large, sumptuous tits. I reached out to fondle one, to feel that perfectly soft yet supple flesh, my thumb teasing her piercing at the pink peak.

"Ah," I moaned. "And all the while you'll be there, on your knees, serving me. Never jealous as I fuck and breed new women?" I asked, doubtful.

"So long as I'm your Chief Consort, and you do not betray me, I will be forever loyal to you, Malchor. I will serve you to my end, at your side," she said, looking up at me with those lidded green eyes before she moved down. Her lips parted and her tongue found the seam of my crown, licking along it with such raw lust.

She was thirsty for me. I'd heard that term, back where I came from, but I never really understood it until I felt her mouth press down on my cock. She was an exceptional talent, and her tongue swirled along the underside of my shaft, tasting my masculinity and caressing the veins that throbbed with hot blood.

"Gods," I muttered aloud with a moan. I lifted my hand from her breast and draped it over her head, caressing those thick locks, taking a firm hold on her but letting her continue to please me as long as it, well, pleased me.

It occurred to me again, why hadn't I corrected her about my name? I told myself that it was because it didn't matter enough to bother. But maybe part of me was afraid that if I corrected her, she'd lose interest. Perhaps she would stop believing I'm this 'chosen one' she seems to think I am.

"You look like a woman who should be a queen more than a consort," I grunted as she tasted my salty pre-cum and worked my manhood into yet another frenzy.

"I don't know what my decision is," I confessed. "I'll know by the morning."

CHAPTER FIVE

I stopped her there, in the middle of the most satisfying blowjob of my life. I felt like a fool doing so, but it was important that I show I was still in control. That even her charms had their limits. So my hand grasped her hair at the back of her head, and pulled her slowly off my dick, until it stood glistening before her eager, pretty face.

"Get some rest," I told her. "You'll need it, no matter what comes in the morning," I said. I sounded so unfazed, so calm and in control.

But honestly, I felt anything but peaceful in that moment. I was a man at war with himself, because nothing would've pleased me more than to have her milk another load from my dick. But I had to show I wasn't some weak-willed man who could be led by the dick everywhere.

Aphaera seemed as surprised and disappointed as I felt. She licked her lips, tasting the remnants of me there before she nodded in agreement.

"As you wish," she said obediently, even though I could smell her sweet arousal thick in the air. She was ravenous for me, but when I let go of her hair, she found a smooth place on the stone floor to lie down. She curled up and watched me curiously for a moment, studying me.

I did my best to look unbothered, and I stretched out to get some rest. Of course, it took a while with my cock raging hard and craving the kind of release only a soft, feminine form could provide. But eventually, sleep did come to me.

By the morning, however, I awoke in much the same condition as I fell asleep: with a raging hard-on. I got up, having grown accustomed to the ache of resting on hard rocks and gritty sand at this point. I peered around, seeing no sign of my little concubine.

I could still smell her in the cave, though, as if my senses had been honed overnight to sniff out her arousal. I wondered if I should take care of myself quickly, just to quiet the beast within and get my control back. I'd managed to push her off of me last night, but who knew how long I'd be able to last like this.

I reached down, wrapping my hand around my own cock, and gave it a gentle squeeze which immediately made me tingle with the urge to unleash the full scope of my lust. Fuck, my shaft felt so huge and stiff in my hand. The male pornstars back home would be jealous of this beast, I realized. I was about to give in and try to achieve my release when a different thought occurred to me: that I should check to make sure she's not close by. As silly as it sounded, after all we'd done together, I didn't want her to walk in and catch me jerking off into the sand, like some horny teen. But more than anything, it was probably the voice in my head that told me: I should never have to jerk off again, not when I have a willing concubine, and the promise of a harem ahead.

Regardless, for one reason or the other, I released my dick and got up. I walked to the mouth of the cave to check and see if my companion was nearby, the sun outside blindingly bright in the early morning.

And it was a good thing I did, because the second I poked

my head out, I saw her returning to the cave. She was just moments away. Close enough that I could see the glint of the sun off her nipple piercings as her enormous tits bounced with each step. In her hands, she held some large green segments of cacti, with the luscious pink fruits placed on top.

"Malchor, you've awakened," she said pleasantly. Her eyes flitted down to my throbbing, hard cock, then back up to my eyes. "You ought to be served if you want to be effective today. Have you made your decision?" she asked, a smile quirking the corner of her mouth. "I'll serve you either way. As a parting gift."

She was too good to be true. Part of me just couldn't believe it. But not the part between my legs.

"Come in out of the sun," I told her as I headed back inside.

I knew she was right. The truth of the matter was that, yeah, I'd definitely need to handle this raging hard-on and all the desires attached to it if I wanted to have a clear head today. Resisting her the previous night had been a calculated move, which I think had the desired impact. But it had cost me something, too, and my sleep hadn't been as restful. The urge for release plagued me all throughout the night.

I stepped back into the cave, and sat down on one of the natural stone slabs again. I looked to Aphaera as she followed after me. I had said I'd take the night to think it over, and the truth of it came to me: how could I pass up a life like the one she offered me? Even if it was mostly bullshit to assuage my ego and she was working some other agenda... wouldn't I have gotten a lot out of it by then anyhow?

I'd have at least gotten my rocks off with the hottest woman around a few times. And likely fathered a child, the idea of which suddenly appealed to me. Especially if I had a dutiful wife--sorry, concubine--to care for the child while I handled the more manly tasks.

"Where did you go?" I asked her, leaning forward with my hands on my knees.

"I wanted to see the position of the sun to better know where we are, and I spotted some cacti not far off. Since you were so *insistent* on thinking things over, I restrained myself from riding you as you slept and procured us breakfast instead. You don't want to get dehydrated. Not out here in the desert," she said, offering me one of the prickly pears and setting the cactus plants down beside me. "I can finish you while you eat," she offered me.

In that early morning light, she was somehow even more gorgeous. She had stripped off the rest of her dress and left herself completely bare except for the sparkling jewels that highlighted her beauty. Her blonde hair was pushed back over her shoulders, and she was thrusting her tits toward me. She bit down on her lower lip, but she restrained herself from touching me quite yet. I could feel the barely-suppressed desire radiating from her.

I studied her, scrutinizing her intentions as well as drinking in her visual perfection. And then I nodded as I took up the cactus fruit, my legs parted wide, to give her access to my hefty balls and thick, hard cock.

"Relieve me," I told her. I drank from that fruit, not letting any of the water inside go to waste as I ravenously began to devour it. We'd been so active the previous day, and in the chaos, I'd lost one of my satchels full of dried meats. "You were obedient. That's good," I told her, in between licking juice from my lips.

There was a sparkle of devious delight in her eyes as she knelt before me, taking my cock in her delicate hands once more.

"I knew it was you, Malchor. You just needed to be unleashed," she said, and then her mouth was around me. She forced herself to take me down deep, but even for all her skills, she was still not able to take me all the way to my root.

I swear, I'd definitely gotten a lot fucking bigger, even compared to just last night. I could chalk it up to being unbelievably hard, but even still, I'd never been *this* thick and long before.

Her hand wrapped around my stem, holding me in place as she began to bob up and down on my cock, her tongue swirling and dancing along my shaft.

Even though I'd interrupted the seduction she had kicked off last night, a full night's rest had clearly done nothing to dampen her apparent enthusiasm for sucking me off. I watched her bob her head up and down my meaty length, unable to quiet my low, rumbling moans as she did so.

"Good girl," I husked, laying my free hand on her head and stroking her silky, golden hair as I continued to eat the watery fruit. "Ahh... we'll need to make some preparations. Our clothes are tattered or outright gone. We'll need more provisions, too. Which means... hunting," I said, trying to talk and plan, while her oral attentions made focusing progressively harder.

She gagged herself on my enormous shaft, her hand gripping my thigh and my cock. Excitement thrilled through her as she fought the urge to pull herself back. Tears formed in her eyes as my cock pressed down the back of her mouth, until at last she couldn't fight it any longer, easing up and freeing up her throat.

She waited just long enough to catch her breath before she repeated the motion, deep-throating me and letting me feel the tight confines of her throat as it fought against my invasion.

I was trying to eat my breakfast, talk out the plan, and enjoy a good blow job. But it was difficult to do even two of those at the same time, so I put the remainder of the fruit down and leaned back to savor the sensations of her mouth and tongue around my cock, enjoying the view.

There was always something special about watching a

pretty woman lick your dick, but with Aphaera, it was extra special. Not just her skill, not just her beauty, but her devotion to the act. How eagerly and enthusiastically she went about blowing me was a sight to behold. If I could've recorded it for all time I would have. But then, it wouldn't be necessary... I would hold this moment in my memory forever. And if she kept up her side of the bargain, I could have this whenever I wanted anyway.

"We can make camp here for a while. I'll hunt, and we'll gather provisions," I said in a husky voice, my dick twitching in her mouth, releasing more pre-cum as I stubbornly insisted on trying to talk through the blowjob.

She couldn't respond with her mouth full of my cock, and that was fine by me. I was the one calling the shots anyway; I didn't need her permission to do what I knew was best.

And she did what she was best at. She worked me up into a frenzy, her hand moving from my thigh to caress my heavy sac. I was already so full and ripe, even after last night, and it felt a little ridiculous. But it felt *good*. It felt *right*. I was a potent man, after all, and I had to be ready to bless any woman with my seed when they begged me for it.

But as macho and full of myself as I felt at that moment, her skill stole my words away. And that was it for the planning. There was no use focusing on anything besides the beautiful woman reverently sucking my cock on her knees. I let my head roll back, moaning and breathing heavily as she worked my shaft and fondled my heavy balls. Just as I began to feel the telltale signs of my impending climax--that fiery tingle traveling up my shaft, the sensation of my balls tightening--she very skillfully and gingerly tugged my sac, prolonging that sensation and making my toes curl as I shuddered.

"Fuck," I panted, savoring the giddy ecstasy of the moment as she drew it out. "I'm gonna... gonna cum," I managed to grunt out as my muscles bulged and tensed, from head to toe.

She had some kind of magic about her, the way she understood my body, and how she craved to bring me such intense bliss.

000When I came, she held me hungrily in her mouth, never letting the seal of her lips on my cock break for a second. She wouldn't waste a drop of my precious seed, as if it was a gift from a God, an elixir of life. She worked my cock until I was completely spent in her mouth. She was having a hard time not letting it dribble out of her full mouth, I'd unleashed so much into her.

"That's it, that's it…" I groaned encouragingly, my hand on the back of her head, keeping her in place. Not that it needed to be. It would have taken an act of god to pull Aphaera away from my cock right then. But eventually I relented, letting her have free rein again. I heaved a mighty sigh, feeling such immense relief.

If you thought blue balls were bad, you should try being left wanting after such a beauty suckled the head of your cock the night before. On top of that unfulfilled need, I seemed to have an even more ravenous appetite for sex than before, a need that was always broiling beneath the surface, even after I finished unloading. It was now a constant drive, a relentless pull. Keeping my urges at bay was practically as necessary as breathing now.

She was careful not to lose any of my cum as she eased off my cock, and swallowed my load while she stared at me with those big, beautiful eyes shining with tears. She looked so gorgeous in that moment, subservient between my thighs, her face still flushed with exertion from having taken me so deep.

I cupped her chin, caressed her cheek with my thumb, and admired her. Funny how I'd thought I was stranded here alone forever only a couple days ago. Now, I knew there were not only other people here, but I had one all to myself.

"You're mine now. I'll keep you. Protect you. You'll care for me and my needs and desires in return. And guide me through this alien world," I said to her.

"Yes, Malchor," she said with a throaty purr, her voice a bit raspy from her over-eager blowjob. I could hear the scratch in her throat and I smell her arousal in the air, but I decided to keep her wanting for now. I wanted her to know who was in control around here, and she seemed to know better than to ask, or even touch herself without my command.

At least for the moment.

"You will eat and hunt, and I will make this place a comfortable spot for us to plan. For you to paint your vision of the future," she agreed.

And so it was. Those first days together were… special, in retrospect. I got to live as a primal man: hunting for food, for hides. Keeping the predators at bay. The Desert Demon remained a threat, but with Aphaera's help we mastered how to walk the desert without alerting it. The one upside to living with that threat was that the shadow beasts were not a problem.

Over the following days, I hunted game. Lizards mostly, and if you think that sounds pathetic, you don't know what this world's lizards could be like.

Some of them were the size of a man. But a few were even bigger.

They made for tough game since some of them spit venom, many had horns and fangs, and all had sharp claws. But I learned how to become the apex predator of the local food chain. So, in no time, our hideaway became adorned with their sleek hides.

We created a flap of hide over the doorway to trap in the cool air during the day and the warm air at night. I found out that she was skilled with sewing. She put together clothing for us both, made from the finest hides I could provide. And oh, did we eat well.

Aphaera tended to things in our hideaway, and gathered up cactus fruit and wild berries that were safe to eat. She had a good understanding of those things, and even knew what flowers and berries to use for seasoning on the lizard meat. So we enjoyed rich, hearty, flavorful fresh food every day. I also practiced methods of smoking the leftover meat to keep for a long journey. Water was the biggest issue at first, but Aphaera unearthed a spring in a nearby cave, and that was more than enough for us.

She taught me about the local area, the peoples and customs. There was so much to learn. In return, I taught her some things about fighting and hunting, and provided better weapons for her. We constructed a bow and some arrows using mainly bones, augmented with feathers from some of the buzzards we managed to snare. (Buzzard was a lousy meat to eat, and so we avoided it except for use in our other crafts.)

But throughout the long days, we found time to wallow in carnality. Once the suns began to set and our bodies were glistening from a day's work, we retired to our increasingly cozy cave-home, where I took my woman in my arms and made use of her in every way I desired.

I was constantly pounding into her tight pussy, her beautiful body on display on her hands and knees. I loved making that thick, bubble-shaped ass quake with each pump of my hips as I rutted into her. I never got sick of that incredible body, never grew tired of stuffing her full of my cock and cum. I never once found my desire waning as we touched, kissed, sucked, and fucked, night after night and often during the day.

It was a miracle she could keep up with me at all, yet she almost always did.

One night as our doggy-style rutting came to a close and I

shot off another big load deep inside her, flooding her depths until my thick, creamy seed was spilling from her puffy folds, I picked her up and we lay down together in the glow of the fire.

She curled into me so readily. I'd quickly come to appreciate her desire for a protector. She could take care of herself, as she'd proven time and time again. But I complimented her skills as she complimented mine. Together we were unstoppable, and she made me feel like every bit the man she told me I was.

"It's a shame to have you waste your seed in me, when you've already sown my womb," she sighed wistfully. "We need to find you another to take your final stroke. We've found comfort and security here, but we mustn't be complacent."

If she was anyone else, I'd have been a little insulted that she didn't want me cumming inside her. But the way she said it made me feel different. I understood it wasn't that *she* didn't *want* my seed. It was that she wanted what was best for me. For my future. For our future together.

"I've consulted the stars, and I believe there is a town over the far ridges of the mountains to the East. We will bring hides to trade, and listen to their problems. And then we will solve those problems, and plant the seeds for what is to come."

Even though I'd just cum, she made me want to go again. All her talk about sowing my seed in many women was tantalizing. But truth be told, I could have been happy in that cave with just Aphaera for the rest of my days. Along with whatever children we made together, of course.

I had grown sentimental. But I don't think, even now, that it diminished me. She was soft and feminine and accommodating. She made my every desire a reality, and I brought her the feeling of safety and purpose she craved.

"We're ready for the journey," I confessed, and kissed her.

"Though truth be told, it's hard to leave this spot, knowing I can have you whenever I want you," I said, squeezing her in my strong arms, making her feel my powerful muscles. "Even if I'm blowing my load without hope of conceiving, it's nice to see my seed drool from your slit, or pour down your face and tits," I said with a grin.

She kissed me back, her full lips so plush against mine as she held me in her arms.

"You speak of such sweet impossibilities," she whispered, kissing my lips, my chin, my throat. "Your temptations rival my own."

"I would be happy to ravage and pound you every day of my life until the very end," I said, leaning back against the stone with an arm beneath my head. I closed my eyes to relax. I was good to go again, but I knew even her astounding body had its limits. I didn't want to leave her overly sore from too much rutting, and I was sated well enough to get some good rest.

"And I'm sure you and I alone could produce a nice few children in time. It'll just take longer," I murmured with my eyes shut, slowly letting sleep take me.

I had been sleeping so well, as I gave into my urges and fucked her every night. The days were long and filled with physical exertion, and that sweet release to top it off kept me sleeping like a baby.

It was still dark when I awoke at the sensation of her hand on my chest, and I saw her green eyes wild and filled with fear.

"They've found us. We have to move!" she insisted.

I had no idea how they'd managed to track us down, only that everything was about to change for good. I'd find out the reason later, but for the moment, I was blissfully ignorant.

CHAPTER SIX

I leapt up from my position in a heartbeat and grabbed for my spear and machete. I looked at her as I prepared to fight and asked, "How many of them?"

"Half a dozen or so," she answered without delay.

"Dammit," I cursed. I pulled on my leather hide armor, a joint project Aphaera and I crafted. It was form-fitting and granted me full movement, but also helped protect some of my more vulnerable areas. "Take care of yourself in here, I'll see if I can handle them," I said.

"We fight together," she said to me, and I had no choice but to nod. And smile.

"We fight together," I echoed back to her before exiting the cave through the hide flap.

I approached the edge carefully, not knowing how close they were. But it didn't take long to find out, because I only narrowly avoided an arrow as it went soaring by and clattered in the stone around me.

"Fuck," I cursed, because an archer was the one element I wasn't 100% sure I could handle in combat. As good as I was in a hand-to-hand fight against these guys, anyone could be felled by a stray arrow from a distance. Even me.

They already had me pinned, but soon the scouts rushed in closer. One was charging at the door, spear in hand, and I deflected his assault with my own spear. But at just that moment, one of them attacked from above the door to the cave.

It was a trap.

The jab of that spear from above was perfectly aimed at me, but luckily Aphaera cried out in the nick of time, "Above you!" and I was able to move aside. I only suffered a cut to my hand that was mitigated by the leather wrap around my wrist and forearm. However, it did make me drop my own spear, so I used my newly-freed hand to grasp my opponent's spear and haul him down.

With a cry, he fell and toppled into his companion. That victory was short lived, as soon, another arrow soared over their heads, intended for me. But once again, I managed to duck to the side and avoid it.

I was tempting fate with every opportunity he got to shoot.

I didn't have time to dwell on it, though, and any plan I could come up with in the moment felt weak. We could retreat inside the cave, whittle them down one by one in the entryway. But that plan relied on them being stupid, and they clearly weren't complete morons. If they had any sense, they'd bottle us up in the cave to wait us out or toss in some burning brush to smoke us out in a single file.

No, we had to stand and fight, take on the offensive. There was just the matter of that damned bowman…

It was then that I watched Aphaera, that perfect beauty, slip past me, her movements utterly agile and fluid.

"Wait!" I called to her, not wanting her to put her life in danger, especially against that archer. But before I could grab her and haul her back behind me, two more of those rough-looking goons came at me.

I used my machete to chop off the pointed tip of one spear,

but had to tango with the other guy, dodging to avoid the slash of his sword.

While I was handling them, I saw Aphaera spring up over a tall rock like some kind of feral cat. It was only then that I noticed the bow in her hands and the arrows in her quiver.

She had moved with such speed and grace, it was hard to put it all together in time before she fired off her own arrow. I heard the blood-curdling scream as she pierced the neck of that archer down below, eliminating him as a threat.

My woman.

She was smooth as silk, and killed with such cold ease it was a thing to behold. It stirred my loins and made me proud of the children we would produce together, especially if they had even a tiny bit of her cunning and agility.

There was no time to dwell, though, as I still had three men on me. Luckily for me, I was not only bigger and far stronger than them, but I also had the advantage of modern steel. My machete cut through their spears like a scythe through wheat. It made them resort to their backup weapons: bone daggers and a crude bronze sword.

One on one, none of them were close to a match for me, but three on one? I was kept on my toes. It was hard to find a moment to strike out, as I was forced to constantly dodge and parry. But my break came when one of them turned to go for Aphaera, and I cut him down from the back.

In return, my magnificent woman put an arrow into the back of another. When it was just me and the man with the bone daggers, I could see the fear in his eyes.

But fear can be a motivating factor as well, and he rushed at me in a flurry of desperate attacks. He forced me to move in such a way that I had to put myself between him and Aphaera, so her arrows were no help, and more than once his daggers slashed at my leather protection. But no matter how deadly he may have been, it was too late for him.

He was going down, one way or another. At the first real

opportunity I got, I cut him right down to size and sent his head rolling to the ground.

Aphaera panted as she looked at me, her eyes wide with fear and exhilaration before she noticed the cut in my leathers. She quickly moved in to inspect it, letting out a sigh of relief as she realized that they hadn't managed to pierce my skin.

She was silent as she continued inspecting me, and when her gaze met mine, it was with a question.

What now?

I stared into her bright emerald eyes and opened my mouth to answer her. But then I noticed it: across the sands was a large party of marauders. Dozens more of those brutes were advancing toward us.

"That was just a scouting party," I told her, by reflex. "We have to move. Grab the travel packs!" I added as I picked up my spear and made my way down the rocks toward the sand.

Luckily, we'd taken precautions. Our travel packs were always loaded with our gear for the journey ahead, in case we had to make a hurried getaway like this. Secondly, I'd set up traps among the rocks beneath our cave mouth to capture foes. The scouting party had managed to avoid most of them, though I did find one triggered and bloody trap to reset.

I looked up and saw them closing in on us, getting nearer in the dim light.

It was too many for us to fight, just the two of us. We had to leave now, buy time, whittle them down. The traps would hopefully help a little, but I knew it wouldn't be enough. So when Aphaera came rushing out with the travel packs, tossing mine to me, I grabbed it and hooked it over my shoulder.

"Let's go!" I said to her as we began to scurry over the rocks in the opposite direction. We had to have a plan here, otherwise they'd eventually track us down and overwhelm us with sheer numbers. There might've been as many as a hundred, and I had no interest in finding out if two could stand against a hundred.

Not personally, anyhow.

We began to make our way across the desert sands, though using the practiced method of moving without rhythm meant that we were much slower than I would've liked. Sure, they had to do it, too, but they also had more archers in the party, and could easily close the gap with arrows.

"I have an idea," I said, not knowing if this idea of mine was going to get us killed or not. I bent down and picked up some heavy rocks. I began to throw them behind us onto the sand, trying to replicate the impact of footsteps as best I could.

When she saw what I was doing, Aphaera joined in and threw a few herself. Just at that time we saw the forces begin to crest over the rocky outcropping of our former home.

"Shit," I swore, realizing we had less time than I thought. We couldn't afford to stand around throwing rocks in the hope of attracting the Desert Demon.

"We gotta put distance between us and them," I said. We hurried as much as we could as I risked glancing back around the sand for any sign of...

There it was, the telltale dust rising up in the distance.

This had to be one of the foolhardiest things I'd ever done in my life, but if it paid off, it would be *epic*.

"There," said Aphaera, catching sight of it just a moment after me, pointing at one of the sand dunes as it began to crater.

Unfortunately, at the same time I could hear arrows whizzing through the sky and landing behind us, much too close for comfort. We had to just pray that the pursuing party was too focused on us to realize a giant devil was lurching in behind them.

Of course, even if we succeeded, we might be next.

"We have to get to the other side before it arrives!" Aphaera said. "Otherwise it might still eat us. Irregular footsteps won't save us when it gets that close," she warned me.

I looked back again as some more arrows whistled past, honing in on us with time. I could see the great cloud of sand getting closer. I could feel the vibrations under my feet. I don't know if it was that same sensation that alerted our assailants, or if it was the way I peered back. Maybe both. But they noticed for the first time that the Desert Demon was edging up on them, and we could hear the distant cries of panic.

I couldn't stare long enough to appreciate it as they fell into chaos. Running every which way, they started to dash back for cover in our camp.

In response, I said to Aphaera, "Fuck it, let's just run!" and the two of us bolted across the sand with everything we had.

I was banking on the fact that a small army was gathered between us and the demon, so that even if it picked up on our footsteps, we'd be seen as dessert, rather than an appetizer. But there was no knowing for certain. "The Demon of the Desert does not think as men do," Aphaera had warned me before.

So we ran, pumping our limbs as fast as possible as we sought to escape the oncoming carnage. As the great demon rising up out of the desert split the dawn with a horrible cacophony of unholy misery, I felt an unnatural urge to look back, to see it.

Aphaera seemed to anticipate this, as she shouted to me, "Do not dare look back, great Malchor! It is not a sight for mortal men!" and I was able to resist.

I'd killed men now, many of them. And I had learned to sleep easy in spite of it. But the horrific screams of men being eaten alive, drawn into its giant maw, would stay with me forever. Theirs was not an easy end, and I'd wish it upon no man. Well... almost.

But they left us no choice. I wasn't going down, not then, not ever.

Aphaera had told me some of the local lore regarding the Demon of the Desert, but even to her, it was an enigma. None had gotten close enough to it and lived to tell the tale, though some claimed they had. But one thing she knew for certain was that it changed a person as it consumed them. It turned them to tar in its maw, its teeth grating the skin, and the screams I heard were almost inhuman.

She'd said that it didn't need to feed the same way we did, and its cycles were erratic. Across some moons, it would be a constant presence stalking the sands. Then it would disappear for years, prompting the townsfolk to think perhaps it had died, until it sprung up again without warning.

Only one Demon had been seen at a time, but there was no sure-fire way to know if it was truly alone, or if they simply took turns. And never had anyone found a cave or lair that the beast might retreat to.

I'd also pieced together that, in this world, there was magic. True magic and real Gods who meddled in the affairs of humans. But every spark of magic or Godly intervention came with a cost, and something told me that the cost of my virility and prowess was not going to be mine to pay.

There was just something about how Aphaera had changed since that first night when we fucked and she'd ensorcelled me. It was hard to put my finger on what it was, but she just seemed more… I don't know. Different.

Maybe I was wrong, but I don't think I was.

I didn't have time to think about it then, anyway. We had to flee once again from the Demon of the Desert, and this time, the mountains were far in the distance. One thing we had on our side was the breaking dawn, though, and the growing light helped me scan the landscape for any place we could hole up and hide before making the rest of the trek.

Unfortunately, all around us was sand and the odd cactus,

so we just had to keep trudging forward, pushing through all the tension in our legs. The screams faded, turning to gurgles of pain and death, and then it almost seemed as though the whole world heaved a sigh. I don't know what it was, not really, but Aphaera and I had to drop to our knees and cover our ears as the intense pressure of that sigh pushed over us.

It reminded me of those old videos I'd seen of a nuke going off. The strange, eerie silence as everything seemed to be frozen in time, and then the exhale as the blast radius grew.

Sand kicked up all around us, biting into our skin. I was grateful for the leather coverings we both wore, but Aphaera had also grabbed the hide we used as a door cover on her way out, and she held it around us, shielding us from the sand.

It must have been less than a minute, but it felt like eternity, as if all my organs were torn from my body then put back in a slightly different place.

We stayed there long after the pressure faded and the sand had fallen back to the earth, and when we finally ventured a look, we saw nothing. No Demon, no army, no nothing.

As if it never happened at all.

There was something about that which sent a terrible chill down my spine.

Don't get me wrong, they were horrible men here to do a horrible thing, and I don't much lament their loss. But there's just something off about the idea of people--any people--being wiped from existence so cleanly, so completely.

After all, if it could happen to them, it could happen to any of us.

That entire group knew that death was a possibility when they came to capture us, but they did it anyway. They took a risk, gambled with their own lives, and lost.

That wasn't something you saw much of in my world, not where I came from. People preferred comfort to risk. Hell, even the richest corporations in the world had stopped trying to innovate and grow, and instead started laying people off and pulling cutbacks to make a little more cash for shareholders. I couldn't imagine any of them putting their life on the line just to kidnap a beautiful woman and me from a cave.

Yes, I was in a completely different world, and I was grateful for Aphaera's soft hand on my shoulder, bringing me back to my new reality.

"It has been appeased," she murmured. "We must continue on, cautiously. We should make it to the ridge by the time the suns hit the mountain peak."

I nodded, feeling a smile tug at the corners of my lips, because no matter how gruesome that fight just was, how close we came to being wiped out ourselves, we survived. And we did it together.

"Let's go," I said. I led us both toward the rock wall.

It was slow going, because we had to be careful with our footsteps again, and there was nothing but rocky, uneven terrain as we approached the mountains. Then, climbing the cliffs was an even slower process. But I still had my climbing pick and ropes, and those helped immensely. I was able to pull Aphaera up as we crested the hills and…

We turned to find a wall of spears pointed right at us. We were caught.

We had a long journey ahead of us, taken as captives by the tribesmen. They'd watched our whole confrontation with the other group from above and lain in wait when they saw us climbing the cliffs. Then they pounced the moment we reached the top.

"They're the Sithia," Aphaera told me, "an independent tribe that refuses to bow to the Warlord-King."

"Well, independent or not, they don't seem too friendly," I

remarked, before the leader of their band told us to drop our weapons and surrender.

"I will drop nothing," I growled back at them, and Aphaera stepped forward with her hands up.

"Listen, we come seeking an audience with your chieftain," she told them, standing so defiant and proud.

Their leader sized her up, scrutinized her.

"And who are you to think yourself worthy of meeting with the chieftain?" he demanded.

"I speak for the great Malchor," she said, and gestured back to me. "We come to offer our services to your wise chieftain. And for a warrior of Malchor's prowess, to forsake his weapons would be a greater shame than death."

They seemed to ponder her words, but finally relented, allowing us to keep our weapons, as long as we kept them sheathed and consented to being surrounded by tribesmen for security.

And thus, we trudged along the rocky plateau for hours beside them.

"Well done with handling that situation back there," I told her.

"This is the only way to meet with the chieftain at this stage of our journey," she said. She wore a slightly apologetic look on her face. "I'd thought we might find another way to speak with them when we were prepared to make an alliance, but they are clever and have traveled farther west than I expected. They know this land well, and they work together against the oppression of the Warlord-King. But I knew your wisdom would temper your bloodlust," she said with an affectionate smile. "I can always trust you to know what to do. But we have little to offer at this point, and it will be more of a challenge to convince him of your greatness."

I wasn't even convinced of this plan of hers: to make me into a new warlord to rival the Warlord-King. But at the moment, we were being pushed along, with little choice about, well, anything. And so we carried on, traveling for hours until at last we arrived at their camp.

The people of the Sithia tribe housed themselves in yurts made from giant bones and lizard-hide, not so different from how Aphaera and I had lived for the previous days. But their yurts were more stylized, as generations of crafting with bone and lizard leather had made them quite skilled with it, and their style was both impressive and imposing.

Although one thing stuck out to me more than anything else: unlike the pursuers who tried to capture us first, the Sithians were not prone to missing limbs or eyes--though some did indeed have battle scars--and they appeared better nourished overall.

"Why do all the men chasing us seem to be missing parts?" I asked Aphaera.

But the captain of the scouting party overheard my question as he came to a stop outside the biggest yurt.

"Because that is the way of the Warlord-King," he said grimly. "All of his subjects are given a choice: serve him, or be maimed to reduce their prowess in battle. So those who do not join his personal army must suffer a missing limb, an eye. Something to cripple their ability to rebel," he said.

"So, wait," I said, looking between Aphaera and him, "you're telling me those men *aren't* part of the Warlord-King's army?"

"Correct," said the captain.

"Right," Aphaera remarked. "Unless the Warlord-King has gotten desperate, they are most likely just bounty hunters, seeking to do his will in the hopes of a reward. They're marked men and it's a risk to shelter them, and often they have a more difficult time on their own. Some become hardened by their solitude and thrive, but others... Others would rather serve the Warlord-King as a Ikput--a fallen son--than continue on their own."

"Damn, that's harsh," I commented, before being ushered inside the yurt.

As my eyes adjusted to the change in light, a low, booming voice chimed in:

"The Warlord-King's methods are always harsh. And so we must be even harsher still," said the chieftain, perched on his throne of bone and hide. He was a big man, almost as tall as me, muscled and strong. And behind him stood a stunning young woman with pale eyes and fiery-red hair.

"Tell me, why have you been trespassing in our territory? Attracting the Ikput that serve that bastard Moloch's will, no less!" he roared. There was anger in his voice as he studied me with a fierce intensity.

But Aphaera moved between him and I, kneeling as she averted her eyes to the floor.

"It was I who led us here, great Chieftain. I was fleeing those assassins when the mighty Malchor saved me from an almost certain death," Aphaera said, and even I half-believed her stretched truth. "We had to flee, to take shelter so that we might heal our wounds and replenish our supplies. We were preparing to depart for Respitine when we were ambushed. Malchor was brave and wise, quickly preparing his own trap for them, to feed our mutual enemies to the Demon of the Desert. It was only our good fortune that brought us to your feet, though I had hoped that when at last we met, we would be able to offer something worthy of your strength and cunning."

I was grateful I had her to handle these sorts of negotiations, so that all I had to do was stand there looking grim and imposing. I could tell this chieftain was intrigued by what she had to say.

"Malchor," the chieftain said, stroking his beard as he studied me, "you do look the part of the Malchor. Not as big as I might've imagined, but... my captain already spoke of your strange weapons." His eyes moved greedily toward my steel weapons, and I had to resist the urge to clutch them possessively.

"You are right," he said after a moment's pause. He cleared his throat and nodded toward Aphaera, though he was looking at me. "It is ill-mannered to come before a chieftain so poorly equipped with gifts…" he added, and again I felt that urge to grab my weapons and keep them in-hand, in case he decided to try and take them from me. I wouldn't be giving them up; they were irreplaceable and invaluable in this world.

"But perhaps there is something else this great Malchor could do for me," he mused, and I didn't much care for his tone of voice.

Aphaera didn't seem fazed, though. She lifted her head just slightly, her voice both seductive and confident when she said, "Malchor can do much, but could do even more with your support. What is it that plagues your mind?"

"There is a great monster that terrorizes my people," the chieftain said, his grin shifting to a grim expression. "Vanquish this creature, and I will entertain your proposals. That is the offer I present to you."

Aphaera was silent for a moment.

"Your people are great hunters. Any monster that could threaten the likes of you is formidable indeed. This gift would outweigh any that we could present you with at the best of times," she said very cautiously. "Our reward would have to match the risk to us, and the benefit to your people."

The chieftain narrowed his eyes at Aphaera, looking irritated. But the girl behind him put a hand on his bicep and it seemed to cool his simmering anger.

"Take the offer, and I will hear your proposal with good humor. That is the deal. What do you say?" he asked firmly, glaring at the two of us.

My woman didn't flinch or seem cowed at all by the harsh stare and the rage clearly bubbling beneath the chieftain's stoic surface. It seemed almost normal to her to negotiate with a man like this. She rose up, looked toward me, then to the chieftain.

"We will need information on your monster, reports from your scouts and survivors, as well as recent sightings and migration patterns. We will review them and develop a plan, and then we will pledge ourselves to your deal."

The beautiful girl behind him leaned in and whispered into the chieftain's ear, and then he softened and spoke once more.

"My scout master will teach you all you need to know. Now go. We have set aside space for you in a yurt for the time being. But do not linger overly long," he said at last, and gave a dismissive wave that brought two of the guards forward to usher us out into the hot sun again.

They guided us to the yurt that was chosen for us, and it quickly became clear this was a place they held prisoners, though we were blissfully spared the indignity of being shackled down.

"You handled that well," I said to Aphaera as I ducked down to get inside.

She smiled at me as she joined my side, seemingly unbothered by the lodgings. She simply settled down and opened her pack, taking out some of the cactus fruit and offering me one.

"It's rarely a wise idea to accept food from a stranger," she explained, "and having something in your stomach will help clear your head and give you some mild protection from any poison, in case we are forced to accept the food or drink."

I looked at her, surprised. She had a way of thinking ahead, for factors that didn't even occur to me. She knew to expect duplicity and treachery at every turn. I took the fruit from her and started to eat. I also took out some of the dried, smoked meat we had packed.

"You're a wise advisor to have," I admired, a smile

tugging at my lips. "What sort of 'monster' do you think they want us to defeat? Something like the shadow beasts? But bigger?" I guessed.

"They are expert hunters, but they do not have the ear of any God any longer. Moloch could not maim them, for they were too quick and cunning, so he damned them to silence instead. If they are struggling with a monster, it would not be one of flesh and bone," she mused.

Her lips glistened as she slowly ate the fruit, her clever mind trying to figure out every possibility, every option. She smiled at me.

"I believe that if we do this, they will be grateful. No chieftain could tell his people that he ousted the man who saved them from a monster responsible for killing their family and friends. And his daughter seems to temper the beast within him well. She will let him see the reason in our request."

I nodded and resumed eating, as my hand found itself upon her knee and thigh. We enjoyed each other's company for a moment longer, before the man who had brought us here appeared at the entryway and came inside.

"The chieftain told me you are going to take up the cause of slaying the monster. That would be good, for it has taken too many from our tribe already," he remarked, crouching down.

He began to draw a map in the dirt. "Here we are," he said, then drew some more landmarks. "And here is where the monster preys. It is over a day's travel from here for a party of two. If you choose to accept, my scouts and I will accompany you part of the way. To ensure you go through with it."

Aphaera moved to the scout's side, looking at the dirt and studying it.

"Does the monster roam?" she asked. I saw the confusion in her eyes.

"It does, aye," he said to her with a nod. "But it always returns to this spot," he said.

He jabbed his finger again at the point he'd mapped out. "That is where it would be easiest to catch it. You do not want to encounter this thing while it is on the hunt," he warned in a grim voice.

"What is its cycle? Does it hunt for food, then nest? How often?"

Aphaera knew all of the important questions to ask that would help us know the beast as well as we could before facing it. But as the scout explained its typical routine of going on the hunt every few weeks, then hibernating, a picture began to grow in my mind of what we were up against.

"It hunts for food, but not like a lizard or a jaguar does. It..." the scout paused, trying to find the right words. "It seems to feed on one's essence. It keeps its catch alive and carries it back to its den."

I listened, but I didn't speak up about what I was thinking. Somehow, I intimately knew that Aphaera was asking the questions so that I would not reveal what my intuition was telling me. Apprehending the beast in its nest, I would find it with a ready source of energy. Whereas, on the hunt, it might be more dangerous because of its hunger. But in its nest, it would be well-fed.

"When was the last person taken? And who were they?" she asked, as if reading my mind. If we could coordinate an attack just before it began to feed, the beast would be at its weakest, but most desperate. It would be a risky wager.

"It hasn't claimed one of ours in over three days. But that's not to say it hasn't eaten since then," he said. "There are other wanderers and traders who pass through our lands at times, after all. The last one of ours it got, however, was a young hunter who dared stray too far on his own."

Aphaera mulled that over before she asked the next and final question.

"What does it look like?"

The answer could never have done justice to what that thing actually was.

CHAPTER SEVEN

Aphaera and I agreed to the offer, and when we told the chieftain he was a little more welcoming. But that really wasn't saying much. His 'welcome' came down to the generous gift of a pillow and blanket filled with buzzard feathers before he promptly sent us back to the yurt.

I had no idea what I was getting into, but the familiar excitement of a hunt was starting to flow in my veins. Could I take down a beast that stalked and preyed upon these strong, seasoned hunters who excelled even in exile? It got me rock hard just thinking about it. Luckily, Aphaera was there, tending to me in her beguiling way.

She was licking my shaft, toying with me, when I caught a glimpse of pale flesh out of the corner of my eye. The yurt had a hide flap for a door that they'd allowed us to shut, but it wasn't a firm seal, and between the seams I spotted a pair of pale eyes.

I grunted and spurted some pre-cum onto Aphaera's tongue as she serviced my manhood. But I looked at those two pale eyes as I gripped my woman's beautiful braided hair.

"You just going to peep all night, or come present yourself?" I challenged in a gravelly voice as my thick, veiny shaft throbbed lewdly.

There was a rustling at the hide flap, as if the spy was considering darting off into the night.

But then the woman entered, the pale moonlight caressing her soft skin. She was wearing a silk gown that fell to the middle of her thighs, her feet were bare, and her fiery-red hair was pulled up into a long, flowing ponytail.

The chieftain's daughter stood before me, watching as Aphaera took me into her mouth, our nude bodies on display. I wasn't stupid. I still kept my weapons within reach.

The young woman didn't seem like a threat, though. She was curvier than the others I'd seen in the tribe. Her tits were heavy, her hips full, and she had freckles across her nose. Somehow, even in the heat of the desert, she remained lily white, her skin almost translucent, which did nothing to hide the blush rising from her chest to her cheeks.

I admit, I took some time to size her up and ogle her, and not just so I could look casual and in control. Sure, that's how I justified it in my mind: act cool, like it didn't bother me that some strange woman was watching me get head. I wanted her to feel intimidated, but it also made for a lovely way to spice up my blowjob.

"What do you want of me?" I asked in a low, growl, made husky by desire. "Does the chieftain want something else?"

She seemed startled by my words, and I felt smug knowing that she was entranced by the sight of Aphaera on my cock. She was being so good, not breaking contact or reacting, just trusting that I could handle this intruder. I figured it was a good test, anyway, to see if that whole harem idea was just sexy talk to seduce me or not.

"No, no," the consort said. She moved in closer to me and knelt down, keeping her voice low. "No one must know I'm here. Please, Malchor, do not give me away to the others. Keep your voice quiet, and listen to me."

Her nostrils flared as she got closer, taking in my masculine scent and making my cock grow even thicker in Aphaera's tight, strained mouth.

I caught a whiff of her own feminine scent, as if a part of me could differentiate her feminine arousal from the mix of scents permeating the air. I nodded as I sized her up, speaking in a low growl.

"Very well. Speak your mind, then, and we will be hush about it," I promised. Aphaera's head, with my hand upon it, continued to bob up and down as I looked at this other woman, as if it were all so natural.

"You will not know the manner of the beast until you see it, no matter how we describe it. But the scout did not tell you all there is to know. The beast is as smart as any man, but faster. It is an expert in camouflage, and can hide in plain sight. Even the bright light of the suns cannot always reveal it. It has tendrils of flesh like a serpent which hide its mouth, filled with teeth like the sand demon's, but not. The hunter we lost did not stray far from the rest. The party he was with said that he was there, then gone the next, as if he was plucked out of thin air."

Her words were disconcerting, and I shuddered at the thought of such a strange, eldritch monster. Or maybe that was just Aphaera's tongue working my sensitive member. Regardless, I listened, then gave the girl a serious look.

"Why are you telling me this? And why would your chieftain keep this hidden from us if he wants us to defeat the monster?" I asked, my bare chest rippling and glistening in the firelight.

"He is a proud man, and needs to defeat the beast for the good of our people. He didn't want to admit how much he needs your help, and he didn't want to frighten you off. But I need you to understand what you're up against, so that you can save us. I will help my father see to it that anything you ask for once this is over is yours," she said.

That lilt in her voice, the way she slightly parted her knees and stared longingly down at my glistening shaft...

It sent a thrill of excitement through me. I could feel that urge to claim her, to seed her and knock her up. Just like Aphaera had told me I would, I wanted it. Needed it. I knew instinctively that this chieftain's daughter was in need of my seed.

I licked my lips and moaned, running a hand back through my hair.

"I'm not going to back down," I told her in a firm voice. "But everything I can find out about this monster will be of aid in the coming fight." I let my steely eyes trail over her slowly, eye-fucking her as Aphaera continued to lick and suck my cock.

She was gorgeous, fuck. She looked like a pristine snow lily in the middle of the desert, except for her flaming red locks and her pale blue eyes that reminded me of an oasis.

But her pillowy tits and thick hips were even more delicious. Where Aphaera was toned and tan, this one was pure softness. And knocking up the chieftain's daughter, well, Aphaera did say that it was a way to establish allies.

Luckily, I still had enough wits about me, even while getting sucked off, to know that I'd take her as my prize, and not to jump the gun. Or perhaps I just realized that Aphaera was working me to my end, and didn't seem ready to relinquish me to this new beauty just yet.

"It's hard to explain how the beast makes you feel. But you must steel your heart against it, ward yourself from its tricks. I believe what they say about you. And when you defeat it, I will give you my sacred prize," she revealed.

My dick twitched at her words. For while she didn't say what her sacred prize was, in that moment, my mind could only conceive of one thing. And I was going to have that.

I took my time, and while grasping the hair at the back of Aphaera's head, I slowly pulled her up off my cock to let it stand glistening and free for a moment so the chieftain's daughter could get a good look at my thick, hard shaft in its fullness. Then I let my woman take control again, and nodded to the chieftain's daughter.

"I look forward to taking your sacred prize when I return victorious, then," I said with a confident smile.

She stared at my cock with such awe and reverence, like a worshipful priestess eager to become a devotee. She shifted, and I smelled more of her heat in the air as Aphaera reached down, caressing my balls.

"Can... Can I stay another moment?" she asked. It was cute how shy she was. Her cheeks were burning bright red, and her nipples were hard as pebbles beneath her silk night dress.

I let my eyes shut to savor the sensation of Aphaera's masterful tongue, and the fact that I was being watched while she did it. But I soon opened them again to look at that ravishing young woman.

"If you bare yourself to me as you sit there, then yes," I told her in a firm, growling voice as my eyes undressed her. My broad chest heaved as I instructed her, "Show me what you have beneath your clothes,"

Her eyes widened, her wet lips parting in surprise. She looked at my cock, then at my face, before she slowly stood up. Old me might have thought she was going to leave, that I'd been a brute and pushed too far. As for the new me? Yeah, the new me wasn't surprised at all when her fingers went to her shoulders and let those sleeves drop.

Her dress was loose, and as she let it fall to the ground, her curves were on full display. I swear, her tits were bigger than my head, and her soft hips... I couldn't wait to take her from behind, to see her thick ass slapping against me. She was a pristine goddess, her skin completely unblemished but for a smattering of freckles here and there.

And her pussy...

Fuck, it was so swollen, so pink, so wet. Between her sumptuous thighs, I could tell how needy she was for my hard cock. She stood there letting me drink her in as Aphaera sucked me closer to finish.

It helped to have such a ravishing new sight before me. I had certainly not grown tired of Aphaera's body, her pleasures. But there was a new thrill in watching this obedient young woman bare herself to me, ogling her body with intense desire as she stood there and watched my pleasure.

"Touch yourself," I commanded. "Lift a breast, play with it. The other hand between your thighs," I rumbled, taking control of the situation and crafting my own little fantasy as I got sucked off. Beat the hell out of jacking it to porn on my phone.

She hesitated again, but she didn't want me to tell her to leave, that much was clear. Because after a moment, her hand groped her pendulous breast, lifting it towards me. Her brows knitted in desire and frustration as her other hand slid between her wet pussy lips. She let out a sigh before biting her lip to avoid making more noise.

I grunted as my dick twitched and released more pre-cum, my balls beginning to tighten as the end approached. But I savored the moment, watching this chieftain's daughter toy with herself somewhat shyly. I couldn't help but lick my lips.

"Good," I rumbled after a long delay. "Squeeze that breast, tease your areola… imagine what it would feel like to be split by my cock as you do," I commanded her.

Her head tilted back a little as her dainty hand worked its way up. Her fingertip traced over her areola and made it stiffen, as her other hand rubbed her clit. It was such a tortured expression that she wore, her face twisted with longing and need in such a wonderful way.

I was going to make sure that she was horny as hell by the time I claimed her virginity, I knew that much.

Aphaera eased up on my cock a little, just enough to let

me draw my orgasm out. Her head moved back, her tongue bathing me as her eyes met mine.

"Do you want to show her what it'd be like or leave it to her imagination, my King?" Aphaera asked in a honeyed voice.

King. I liked the sound of that suddenly, though I never had before. I smiled wryly down at Aphaera, before looking to this willing, eager young chieftain's daughter.

"What do you say, girl? Do you feel up to seeing what it would be like?" I asked her. I trailed my tongue along my lips slowly as my dick leaked pre, adding to the glistening sheen of saliva that Aphaera had left upon it.

She was transfixed by my cock, and she moved closer as though I had cast a spell on her. It was intoxicating.

"Can I touch it?" she asked, coveting the place of Aphaera's hand still wrapped around my thick stem.

"You may," I answered in a low rumble, looking from this girl to Aphaera, surprised at how much I enjoyed this game she'd set in motion. "But you will not feel it inside your 'prize' until the time is right. So don't get too ahead of yourself," I cautioned her as my cock throbbed before her eyes.

The chieftain's daughter knelt before me, taking her hand from between her thighs and wrapping it around my wet cock as Aphaera relinquished her position.

"It's so... big," she said with surprise in her voice. Then she jumped a little as my cock pulsed, the veins throbbing against her palm.

"Oh! It jumped!" she said, and Aphaera giggled a little.

"It does more than that," Aphaera said, shifting her body to straddle me with her ass resting on my abs. "You hold it right there," she instructed as she moved forward, lifting her hips and positioning herself over my dick until her pussy lips kissed my crown.

"Say when, Malchor," she purred over her shoulder at me.

In the time since we met, Aphaera and I had learned to

move as one. Our fucking was glorious, the stuff that would put porn to shame. She was toying around, putting on a little show for the new girl as I reached out and grasped her hip.

"Keep a firm hold on my cock," I growled to the redhead. "Aphaera here is quite tight. And if you don't keep it in your grasp tightly it won't work," I said. I licked my lips, then gave Aphaera's bubbly ass a smack.

"Do it," I said with a twinkle in my eye for my beautiful Aphaera, watching her instead of the amateurish new girl.

Aphaera speared herself on my cock until her juicy pussy was tightly pressed to the other woman's hand. She stayed there, grinding on me, as her fingers took the woman's chin and guided her mouth toward her.

Their kiss was the stuff of fantasies. Aphaera's tanned skin met her beautiful pale flesh, their mouths opening as Aphaera's tongue teased along her lips, tasting her with delight.

They lingered for a second before Aphaera's hips lifted and crashed back down, her pussy squeezing me tight as she begged for my cum.

Suddenly, only was I having my cock ridden by the hottest woman I'd ever seen, I was glimpsing the whole future Aphaera had promised me. Aphaera, tending to my every whim and desire, with other beautiful women at my beck and call. I moaned aloud, restraining nothing as Aphaera pumped my cock. My hands gripped her hips and gave her ass another spank in reward. But my eyes were locked on the sight of the two girls making out as I shivered with delight.

"Beautiful… beautiful sight," I husked appreciatively, my body tensing up as I held back my climax just a bit longer, wanting to continue savoring that sight.

Aphaera's hand tangled into the girl's fiery red hair, pulling her in and holding her in place as they kissed deeper this time, a moan traded between their mouths. Aphaera was so wet on my cock, soaking the other woman's hand, and getting wetter by the second.

Aphaera's fingers went to the other woman's sex, playing with her, but not letting herself press inward.

"I want you as tight as possible for our King," Aphaera whispered to the other woman as she played with her clit.

My hands on Aphaera's waist and ass gripped her tighter, and used the leverage to buck her up and down my cock faster. My moans filled the yurt, my body glistening with perspiration like Aphaera's, the thin sheen highlighting our every curve, every rigid muscle.

"How does she feel? Worthy?" I asked my obedient Aphaera as her body slid up and down my shaft, milking my cock with that tight, expert flow.

"She feels like silken ecstasy," Aphaera said as she lifted her fingers and licked the other woman's honey from them. She leaned in, giving the woman another long, languid kiss as her pussy squeezed me, craving my gift.

I was getting so achingly close, but I didn't want it to end. Not my first time fucking multiple women. But Aphaera was a master of sensuality, and my dick was aflame with intense sensations.

I reached out with one hand to caress over the pale beauty's figure, down her side and back, across her freckled skin so smooth and flawless. I groaned, then slid my hand around to cup one of her breasts. I squeezed and teased it, letting my thumb swirl around her nipple, feeling that stiff protrusion.

"F-Fuck," I grunted, feeling my time was at an end. My cock was throbbing wildly, and I tilted my head back and my eyes rolled with pleasure, moaning lewdly as I came.

Aphaera took me in as deeply as she could, with the other woman's hand still grasping me tightly. It was such a fucking thrill, getting to see and feel those two beauties serve me with such devotion and need. Their moans were sweet music together, their kisses frantic and clumsy as my shaft swelled even thicker and I unleashed my load.

Thick blasts of creamy white seed flooded into my dear Aphaera, filling her already-claimed womb. I twitched and jerked, my cock swelling thickly in the new girl's hand, while I squeezed her breast and savored that soft flesh.

I knew then that I was an impressive man. The biggest, mightiest, hottest man in this wild world. I knew it because these two women made me feel it. The way they tended to my desires, the way they milked my cock, held it with such reverence.

"Fuck, fuck yes," I grunted as pulse after pulse of creamy spunk filled Aphaera to her capacity. My sweet, obedient, skillful Aphaera... I found myself moaning her name aloud without even realizing it.

She rode me through my orgasm, making sure that I would never forget that moment in the dim light of the prisoners' yurt. She'd teased me, tormented me, filled my head with desires I never knew. And she'd promised me more.

When I killed that beast, I would plant my seed again. I was suddenly filled with a purpose greater than any man had ever known.

The pale girl was leaning toward me as if she was about to speak when she froze up. I heard footsteps approaching outside: two men, maybe three, headed in our direction. Her eyes went wide as she grabbed her dress, struggling to fit her curves back into it in such a rush.

"Guard yourself well. I will wait for you," she said breathily before she disappeared into the night, as the last strand of my cum leaked into Aphaera's womb.

We didn't even have time to move off each other, or maybe we just didn't care to, before a scout poked his head in. He started to speak, but his words were cut off as he found Aphaera's beautiful body still grinding on my dick. She giggled when she caught his eye.

"Just preparing for battle," she explained easily. "What is it?"

The man cleared his throat, averting his eyes. "I just wanted to tell you that we'll leave at dawn... if that's okay," he murmured.

"We should be done with our preparations by then," I said with a grunt, giving Aphaera's ass another clap with my big, strong hand. Then I flashed a grin at the scout, increasingly shameless about my body and its carnal acts. "Right, Aphaera?"

"Might be tight, but we'll make it," she giggled again, seemingly in good spirits at how things were going so far. She lifted up on my cock again, then fell down upon it, making her tits jiggle.

I slid a hand up from her hip to cup a breast while the other gave her ass another slap, before grabbing hold of her and pumping her up and down on my cock again with renewed vigor. I was so full of bravado and even more cum to unload, I just started rutting into her all over again, with the vigor of a teenage boy.

"We'll be there," I told the scout, huffing and panting as the wet sounds of our bodies slapping together filled the yurt.

Of course, as confident as I was at that moment, I had no idea of the hellishly fearful creature I was about to confront on the dry plains. Or the cost of confronting it.

CHAPTER EIGHT

e were up at dawn, after I fucked Aphaera senseless for much of the night. Despite the exhaustive rutting we engaged in, it never seemed to tire us however. We just got up, prepared our things, ate well, and set off.

As we were leaving the camp, I spotted that pale beauty watching from just outside of the chieftain's tent. Her soft body was draped in a gossamer robe, and she wiggled her fingers at me, a silent wish of good luck before she went back to her father's side.

The journey ahead promised to be long: a whole day's travel across hot, arid plains. But I had Aphaera by my side, the two of us flanked by scouts, and all of us keeping an eye out.

"Be wary, the monster sometimes hunts far from its den; it could be anywhere," the scout leader had warned us.

I still remembered what the chieftain's daughter had said about the beast possessing powers beyond normal reason, and it made sense. Aphaera had said that magic was their weakness, so I figured that magical camouflage was probably what we were dealing with. Not that I knew how to deal with magical camouflage, but I was cocky enough to believe that I'd figure it out when the time came.

"The air changes when magic is present," Aphaera said, reminding me of when the Demon of the Desert snuffed out all those lives. It sounded like we might be dealing with a similar problem, so I tried to rely on my sensory memory of that day more than my usual mundane sense of tracking.

As we advanced farther across the sun-scorched plains, I was grateful that at least that we were no longer treading on desert sand. The stuff got everywhere, it burned the soles of your feet, it was just awful.

But the further along we went that day, the more anxious and on edge the scouts became. They knew what lurked out there, and they were not eager to go anywhere near it.

We stopped but once that day for a brief bite before sunset then we carried on. It wasn't until dusk was blanketing us that the scouts' called to set up camp.

"We will prepare a feast, for this is as far as we go. After tonight, you head the rest of the way on your own," said the scout leader to us.

Aphaera set up work to get ourselves comfortable, pulling out some of our own supplies in a stealthy manner and leaving some dried meat out of sight of the scouts. We were all on edge and didn't have much to talk about. But maybe after I killed this beast, I could trust them a little more. After all, I was going to do what their chieftain couldn't.

I hoped.

It would really suck to have my essence slurped up by a monster in the desert before I got a chance to cast my seed to the four corners of the world.

I took a final look around, scouting the perimeter of our camp before coming back to Aphaera. I settled in next to her, and the two of us ate well and talked of what was to come. I relied on her for insight, her clever mind always working in ways that others' didn't. She was generally able to see several steps ahead, and I'd need that.

"We will be victorious and on our way back in no time," I assured her, with a kiss to her forehead and a caress of her long, pale hair.

"Yes, breeding the chieftain's daughter would go a long way to securing your claim against the Warlord-King," she said, but she sounded a little distant. Thoughtful.

"What is it?" I asked, crouching next to her.

She frowned, shaking her head.

"I'm not certain. I feel as though I've heard of a beast like this before, but I can't remember where. Something about serpents covering a mouth," she let out a soft sigh. "Regardless, you should eat and clear your head before we rest. I'm sure the scouts won't mind our little display. Perhaps it will come to me."

I grinned at her, caressed her hair, and leaned in to kiss her cheek and neck.

"If fucking while all these scouts watch from a distance doesn't jostle the thoughts from your head, I don't know what will," I said, before sliding my hand inside her leather bra and fondling her breast.

We rutted for the rest of the evening as our hosts watched, cheered, and enjoyed the sight. Aphaera screamed her pleasure into the night, helping give them a show to remember before we finally lay back, my woman clinging to my chest as we drifted off into sleep.

It never did come to her, whatever folklore she'd half remembered. But there would be time enough for that in the morning.

I was still pretty out of it when I caught the scent of the chieftain's daughter, and my nostrils inhaled it greedily. I thought it was a dream so I kept my eyes closed, wanting to see where it went.

I felt her soft, delicate hands on my chest, her skin

unweathered by the elements or hard labor. She was a pampered girl, spoiled by her father, and I was reaping the rewards.

"I can't wait for your success," she whispered in my ear. Her large breasts touched my chest as she began to climb on top of me. "I need to feel you. It was so cruel to have left me wanting like you did."

My cock stood at attention and throbbed against her thick ass.

I had been intent on waiting to secure my victory before claiming her as my rightful prize. But with her atop me like that, her body so soft and delightful to touch… I just lifted my hands to slide up along her thighs, to her hips and ass, and let loose a long, low rumble of need.

"Greedy girl," I growled. "You just can't wait to have your little pussy deflowered and filled, can you?" I rumbled, as my cock pulsated wildly with desire. The damn thing was insatiable these days. As long as there was a woman on hand to stuff it into, it never wanted to go down.

She whimpered, her body writhing amateurishly on top of me, her breasts pressing into me as she lifted her hips. My shaft bobbed under her waiting pussy, slapping against her wet slit, and she let out a moan into my ear.

"You just looked so big, so filling," she purred, wriggling on me. "I want you to teach me what you like. I want you to mold me into your perfect plaything."

It was so comfortable lying there, letting this horny young woman paw and purr at me. So I languished there a while, letting her have her run of things as I caressed her smooth, soft flesh, savoring her virginal beauty before I finally deflowered her for good.

"Oh, I will," I rumbled to her in response. My cock pulsated and spurted pre onto her body. "You'll be my sweet pet for all time, and never have eyes for another," I promised her.

I squeezed her ass and slid another hand up to fondle her breast. "No cock but mine will ever satisfy you after you've had it," I boasted.

Her nipple was so hard between my fingertips, and her back arched to push up into me more as she kept grinding awkwardly against my dick. She didn't know what she was doing, but her soft body was pleasing all the same. Especially since I knew what I had to look forward to. Well, not exactly. I'd never had a virgin before, but I had an exceptional imagination.

She reached behind her, finding my thigh, but she couldn't turn far enough to grab my dick without me relinquishing her tit, and I wasn't ready for that yet. I held onto her, yanking her back toward me.

"Put your tit in my mouth," I ordered, and within seconds I was practically suffocated by breast flesh, her nipple poking against my lips. I lightly took it between my teeth, forcing it to harden even more before I started teasing it with my tongue.

She moaned so loudly I knew that she was going to wake Aphaera, and I wanted that. I wanted my girl to watch this.

I wanted Aphaera to be a part of my deflowering this girl, to be a part of it all. A man needs a woman at his side at all times: someone who'll have his best interests at heart. Someone to share all things with. Including his harem.

I thought of that as I suckled that supple teat, fondling the pale flesh up and down her figure with my two strong, greedy hands. Gods, she was so soft and pleasing to the touch, and my dick was pulsating hard and fast with want. If I let myself, I'd unleash on her with a terrible fury of lust.

I grabbed her hip, pushing her toward my cock, and felt that silken wetness begin to coat me as I sucked her tit. She was mine. She would do anything I said. She sneaked all this way just for me to fuck her, to take her virginity. I throbbed so hard, and her hips lifted just at that moment for my crown to connect with her waiting hole. I moaned against her nipple, and she started trying to get my cock to pierce her tight, virginal pussy.

I let her breast go, blowing on it to make it tingle. I opened my eyes, looked to Aphaera, and found her fingering herself.

But her mouth was open, waiting for something to enter it. And that was when I saw it.

It.

There were no words for this thing, the tentacles made of serpents heading straight for my beauty's mouth as if it were a cock. I went to push the chieftain's daughter from me only to realize that there was nothing there. Nothing but air.

An oppressive, sticky, pungent air like hot tar weighed down on me.

I should've realized something was up sooner, like how strange it was that I didn't want to open my eyes. But it was like a dream, and the rules of reality hadn't been working in my favor. Dammit… I cursed myself for being so lax. I shouldn't have trusted the scouts setting up watch around us.

But as I gazed upon that hideous monster, its mass a writhing heap of snakelike tentacles, its body an oily black mess of eyes and maws, it broke a part of my brain just to look at it. The thing was suspended there on centipede-like writhing limbs, but also seeming to… hover in the air, as if it had no weight. There was no way the few limbs that touched the ground like a gentle caress were actually holding it up; it was some magic creature that disobeyed gravity itself.

Part of me felt the urge to run, part of me was frozen in terror at seeing something that should not exist. But the far greatest part was ready to fight, so I grabbed the machete that lay beside me, never far from my reach, and I sprang up.

"She's mine!" I bellowed as I cut down through the serpentine mass that was about to defile my Aphaera, leaving it to twist and hiss on the ground, severed and dying.

There was a terrible cry, but instead of it filling the night, it filled my head. I could feel it inside of me, clawing and thrashing, but I was able to keep my mind clear. That only seemed to make it more enraged, and one of those snake tendrils lashed out at me, fangs poised for my wrist that held the machete.

Aphaera moaned, her fingers slipping inside her creamy pussy, still stained with my seed, and she licked her lips.

"Malchor, I need you," she moaned.

She was completely out of it, lost in some illusion this creature created like I was. Maybe she just needed a shove, something to awaken her. So as I dove out of the way of that striking snake-tentacle, I scooped Aphaera to come with me, and the two of us tumbled across the plains, her body under my arm to protect her from harm.

But as we came to a halt, I could see she was still deep in that trance, lying there beneath me. She was moaning and fingering herself still, muttering my name.

"Dammit," I cursed, getting up before this thing could pounce again. I had to keep it away from Aphaera until I could figure out how to slay it.

I jumped up and prepared to fight, its many maws screaming at me in an unearthly rage. I slashed my machete at another of its approaching snake-limbs, and severed its head. But the next one retracted in time, dodging my assault.

It was then I noticed that some of the scouts were standing. Two of them were approaching, with weapons in their arms. But any relief I felt was momentary, because their gaits were awkward and slow. They wielded their spears… oddly. I realized what they reminded me of: zombies, from some horror film.

They were under the monster's control too, locked in some illusion or dream that made them think they were battling some foe. Or the monster itself.

I didn't want to hurt them, so I dodged their first attack. Then I bounded away, trying to circle the monster to put it between scouts and myself. But in the process, the hideous monster renewed its own assault, and I saw from amid its mess of maws and eyes one big eye flickered open with a sickening 'shlick' sound, staring right into me.

I could feel the burning sensation of its powers trying to take hold of me. There was a nagging sensation at the back of my head, as if my mind itself was growing hot and fiery. But I resisted its attempt, and I renewed my assault.

Truly, I wanted to lodge my machete into that big eye. But the many writhing snake-limbs prevented me from doing that right away. I had to dodge and parry their strikes, while also doing my best to keep distance between the scouts and me.

It was not going as planned, to say the least. Even worse, I was still raging hard from my hot dream, so I had to be doubly protective of that. Aphaera's sweet moans were doing nothing to tame my own beast, which was dangerous because the situation was definitely not helped by so much blood flooding my other organ instead of my brain.

Fuck, being so virile could be a real curse at times.

A spear came at me from an angle I wasn't expecting, and I only swung moved my machete in time to parry it. Of course, my steel blade cut through the wood or bone it was made of in the process, and left it without a tip.

"Bill me for it later," I muttered aloud, as I kicked the man who wielded it, knocking him to the ground on his ass.

I curved my blade back around and hacked off two more of the beast's writhing limbs, causing it to scream in agony again. But this time, it didn't retreat or play it safe. It grew bold. Desperate.

It lunged, biting and glaring at me, pummeling me to the ground with a surprise assault and knocking my machete from my hand.

I looked and saw my weapon out of reach. I cursed beneath my breath as I instead had to grab at a snake-tentacle, grasping it by the neck to keep it from biting into me.

It glared down at me with hate and malice, and then with its final viper it lunged again. I moved my head just in time, and it bit into dirt, which gave me the chance to grab that one, too. I shoved a knee up into its mass, feeling its many small, sharp-fanged mouths biting into my leather. But it was more important I kept its bigger mouth away from biting my head off.

In that moment, my certainty wavered. I wasn't sure if I'd make it. I was overwhelmed, and I could glimpse the other zombie-like scouts advancing to aid it, in some delusional state that made them think I was the enemy.

This was the kind of moment in which I really could've used Aphaera stepping in to save my ass, like she had a habit of. But a glance in her direction showed that she was still lost in her dream, fingering that tight pussy, moaning my name out into the night.

I thought it might all be over as I watched those asps bite at the air, trying to get to me, the main maw gnashing with rows upon rows of sharp, jagged teeth…

CHAPTER NINE

As I struggled in a battle of raw strength with that monster, I pulled at its remaining snake-limbs, straining them, making them hiss in agony.

I was going to rip them out with my bare hands, I swore then and there. I could feel the snakeskin tearing as I gritted my teeth and growled. But the creature raged on, pushing in on me harder, more urgently.

My response? A headbutt, right into its big fucking eye, sending it reeling. It tore back and caused those snake-limbs to rip away from its body into my hands.

Its hideous screams filled the night, but I leapt up, grabbed my machete once more, and ran at it as it staggered away, hovering in the air. I let loose a booming war cry and charged right for it. I jumped and slashed down with my machete, cleaving that monster's bloodshot eye open.

I had no idea what the liquid was that sprayed out from it, and it's honestly best I don't think too much about it. It shouldn't exist, whatever it was. It defied reality. Sure, the usual mixture of pus and blood and innards was arguably gross enough, but this was worse than all that. It burned through my leather, and I had to stagger back, ripping my arm-cuffs off and tossing them to the side as they disintegrated. Then I got way the fuck back as the thing started lunging toward me again, spraying its deadly venom into the air erratically.

I guess the pain was enough for it to lose its mind-control abilities on the others, though, because I heard them start to mutter in confusion behind me.

"Stay away from its blood! Arrows!" I shouted.

I dodged as it clumsily lunged at me again, that scream echoing in my skull and setting me off balance. I fell to one knee, then rolled to my side, a glob of blood sizzling into the stone beside my head.

That had been way too close. I needed to get some distance.

I didn't think about it, I just acted, darting to its side beneath its torso, hoping to use the creature's own body as a shield. Then I felt an arm reach out, nails digging into my shoulders, a burning sensation making me lose control of my sword arm. My machete dropped and I was unable to pick it up.

And then finally, blissfully, I heard those arrows sing through the sky and the beast raged, letting me go.

Or, well, its claw let go, as an arrow pierced through it, severing the nerves.

Aphaera fired another arrow, then another, not letting up. She was stunning, still glistening from her mind-controlled fantasies, her body nude in the silver moon as she readied another arrow, letting it sail through the sky.

The scouts were slower to come to, though, confusion still rendering them useless to us, but at least they weren't actively fighting *me* anymore.

Aphaera was all I needed on my side. I jumped and rolled, grasping my spear up. I spun around and found the thing screaming and spewing bile in my direction as it lunged. But I didn't run, I charged back at it in turn.

And as my woman stuck him full of her arrows, bleeding life from it with each new strike, I charged in and struck the finishing blow. My spear sank in through its burst eye, exiting out the other side of its mass to dig into the ground.

I stood over it triumphantly as it finally went still, a gory, hideous mess beneath me as the scouts looked on in shock, amazed that I'd managed the impossible.

I did it.

I did it!

Its poison ate through the earth and I backed away, not taking any chances at getting that fluid on me. I was planning to take it back with me as proof that I had succeeded, but then I saw its flesh begin to bubble. The corrosive toxin seemed to even be eating away at its own body, forming a puddle of black, wicked sludge that filled the air with its stench.

But as the final bit of it rotted away, the air softened around us, and the sounds of the arid land slowly began to return. One small gemstone-like object at the heart of the monster remained, and I carefully reached in and grabbed it up, stuffing it into a pocket to study closer later.

Aphaera's tits pressed against my arm as she hugged me, staring on in wonder.

"I was trapped in that dream, but you saved me," she said with such awe.

I put a strong arm around her, holding her tight against my side with my hand on her ass. She was my girl, all mine. And I liked to make that clear with every touch as the awe-inspired scouts watched.

"I know," I said, smiling confidently down at her before helping myself to her lips with a deep, passionate kiss. "I'll always save you," I promised.

And all around us the scouts broke into cheers of excitement and victory, for the scourge that had been hunting their tribesmen was now gone.

I beamed at Aphaera, then at the scouts, lifting a hand into the air in celebration. Fuck, it felt good to be a badass!

I was already forgetting what life used to be like: sitting in a dreary office, saving my money to go on the next spelunking trip. Why would I want to think about that, when a hot girl was holding me close, a ton of expert hunters were cheering me on, and my dick was thicker, longer, and harder than ever?

"We should return to claim your prize," Aphaera purred to me. "I'll help you get a bit built up for her first time."

I grinned down at her, so drunk on victory, on her sweet, adoring words and the way she set me up to be a King. I kissed her again passionately and fondled her bare breasts before the men, who were still cheering, and then pulled back enough to speak once more.

"I would relish celebrating my victory with you right here, right now. But you're right," I said, slowly loosening my grip around her body.

"Come. Get dressed, and let's head back. The tribe will celebrate our news!" I said with a shout to everyone, who whooped and hollered with us, filling the early morning dark sky with our cries of victory.

The trek back was faster than the one out, as everyone was full of such cheer and excitement. Plus, the need for a careful march wasn't as high now that we knew the monster was defeated and gone for good. I got many admiring looks, thanks, and congratulations even before arriving back.

"How did you do it?" the scout master asked, respect heavy in his voice. "I was standing watch when one of the others relieved me, and then..." he trailed off, sounding confused. "I couldn't pull myself out of it, no matter how hard I tried."

"Once I noticed something about the dream felt off, I just pulled myself out of it," I said with a shrug of my broad shoulders. Aphaera was on my arm, sneaking a touch of my manhood now and then, keeping me primed and riled up. "It took willpower, but willpower was what I had," I said.

Though in truth, I feel like I got the least of it. The others were made to be like playthings for the monster. But it seemed like its influence over me ended as soon as I opened my eyes. Even then, I pondered that maybe I was different. Special. Because I wasn't from this world, and therefore wasn't susceptible to its strange magic.

Aphaera had said that their weakness was magic, so maybe that was how she was able to come to my aid more quickly than the others. But for me?

Yeah, it was as easy as opening my eyes.

I smirked a little as the scout master stared at me, nodding his head. He fell back a little, following behind me, back where he belonged. I might still be learning the land and its people, but the people were learning their place, too.

Following me.

When we arrived back, the tribe looked on with wide eyes. They didn't cheer, they didn't say anything at first. The reason soon struck me: they assumed we'd come back early, having given up. Because none of our numbers were missing, and it hadn't even been a full two days since we left.

But the scout master raised his voice and gestured to me.

"The hero Malchor has defeated the monster! Our hunting grounds are free of its tyranny again!" he said

A great wave of relief washed over the tribe. Faces lit up, some cried, some embraced. Many rushed before Aphaera and me, fell to their knees and gave thanks.

The chieftain came out from his yurt, his gorgeous daughter not far behind, and her pale eyes lit up at my return. At our triumph!

Her fingers slid over her bodice, over her nipples, and she caught my gaze as she played with herself for a second, knowing that she was invisible as all the tribe stared at me.

The memory of my dream was still thick in my mind, and my shaft stood at attention beneath my thick leathers.

She licked her lips, biting down on one corner, and Aphaera purred in my ear, "You will ask for him to give his daughter to you and swear himself to your cause. They are free to live their lives, but she will carry your child, and you will return to him when you need his services to defeat the Warlord-King."

I squeezed Aphaera's ass as she gave me instructions, then released her from my arm as I strode on up to the chieftain. He was a stern man, big and imposing. But he couldn't help but crack a smile as we approached him amid the cheering masses.

"Your task is done, chieftain," I said to him, my voice deep and strong. "The monster is dead. And your people will face no more challenges from it."

He looked like he was about to question me, but the head scout pushed up front and interjected with a grin.

"It's true, chieftain! We all saw it! The monster put us under its spell, but the Malchor was impervious. He rose up while the rest of us were ensorcelled, and in a bloody battle, he slayed the great tyrant!" he said, as more cheers erupted all around.

I could tell the chieftain wanted to take our conversation inside, so we entered his yurt again. Some of the tribesmen followed in too, crowding the place, to hear what was to come. The chieftain had clearly wanted privacy, but he knew to deny his people a part of this conversation would rankle them. So he sat back in his seat and looked me up and down.

"You are every bit the Malchor. The prophesied warrior-general," he said. There was some reluctant admiration in his voice, but the tribesmen surrounding us were giddy with excitement. "Then your part is done. And it falls to me to ask: what is it you wish, great Malchor?"

I stood tall. The only one daring to stand near me was Aphaera, and she kept behind me, letting me lead.

"I want your tribe as my ally. Live as you wish, I will not meddle, but..." I said firmly, my voice full of calm and control, "when the time comes, I will cast down the Warlord-King, and end his despotic reign. With your help," I said, which garnered more cheers from the people. It was clear that was exactly the kind of thing they wanted to hear, because they sounded even more excited than they had for the death of the monster.

Of course, for my part I hadn't even really decided if I wanted to do that. It had been Aphaera's plan, but I hadn't come right out and said it was mine either. But now... I guessed I was in.

"That is a big request," the chieftain said, his brow furrowed in thought. Unlike his people, he was concerned with the ramifications of my bold proposal.

"And to solidify our alliance," I went on, my eyes drifting from the chieftain to his beautiful young daughter. "Give me your daughter. She will become one of mine. A symbol of our bond," I said, locking eyes with her still.

He was considering the first offer, but at the second, a fire touched his eyes and he reached for his weapon. But then his daughter's hand was on his shoulder, and she leaned in, whispering to the chieftain.

He looked at her with pain in his eyes, before that softened away and he sighed.

"I suppose you are not my little girl any more, Nyphenah, but this..." he trailed off. She leaned in, kissing her father's forehead.

"I will pledge myself to you, Malchor, the demon slayer," she said, her delicate voice filling the room. The tribe seemed to know better than to take her word for it, though, and they waited for the chieftain to weigh in.

Nyphenah. I stared at her, watching the graceful way she

moved and her soft curves, and in return she stared back at me.

"If it is what she wants, I will not deny her," he finally said. "But we will not be pawns in your army, easily discarded. If we are to be allies, then we will be true allies."

The chieftain stood once more, sauntering toward me. "And when the Warlord-King lays dead at our feet, we will part, and you will allow us to continue to live as we do. No man or woman or person in this room will go against you, and you will not go against us. Let it be told."

I stood strong, and while the chieftain was the tallest member of his tribe, I was the biggest man in the room. I looked at him seriously, then extended an arm.

"With your daughter as mine, we will be family," I said to him, as we gripped each other's hands, not in a handshake, but as a firm grip of camaraderie. "I will forever think of you all as my kin, and treat you accordingly," I swore, my gaze drifting back to his hot daughter.

Nyphenah.

"Kin. Yes," he said, following my gaze, then meeting my eyes again. "You will care for her as I do. She is delicate. You will protect her."

"He's saved my life many times, Chieftain. And I will help pamper her," Aphaera said. Both the chieftain and I picked up on the seductive lilt to her tone. He bristled slightly before he nodded.

"Good. I will hold you to that. Go now and rest, bathe in the spring. I will prepare Nyphenah," the Chief said, gesturing to the exit. "The rest of you, go, and prepare for the feast! Tonight, we celebrate!"

The kind of night I was in for… well, let's just say I had no idea of what was coming.

CHAPTER TEN

Aphaera and I exited the yurt, and the scouts who once guarded us like captives were now replaced by some maidens of the tribe, who guided us to the spring. There, we got to see the beautiful, flowing water, the lush greenery, the flowers budding in all manner of colors.

"This is a place of holiness," said the woman who guided us there, "and it is cleansing. These items will ensure you are prepared for the ritual of joining," she said, as she laid down a basket full of oils and soaps.

"These are the customary garb of the groom…" she added somewhat more hesitantly, as she laid out the fine white garment.

It was so pristine, which was always a rare sight in this harsh landscape, but when I took it in my hands, it was heavier than I expected. I shifted it, finding that the cloth was attached to a belt made of fine silver metals, inlaid with sapphire gems. It seemed like a sort of kilt that was open on one side to reveal my right thigh.

I put it back down and smiled at the maiden as I began to undress, my cock lewdly throbbing in the golden light of dusk.

"Thank you. You may stay there and apply the oils once Aphaera is done bathing me," I said as I stepped into the spring.

Aphaera laughed, flicking me with her fingers as she stripped out of her leathers and put them aside. "You're going to torture the poor girl," she chided me, but I could tell that she loved it. She quickly stepped into the water, grabbed the soap, and began to run it over my skin.

"I can apply the oils," the maiden said, giving us both a smile. "I do not mind."

"Of course you don't," I said with a confident smirk

I relaxed back in the spring, enjoying the feel of so much clean, free flowing water. I hadn't experienced anything like it since I'd entered this world. The last time I'd been around enough water to submerge even one entire limb was back on Earth, in that strange cavern I'd so foolishly climbed into.

My cock twitched as I felt Aphaera clean my body, and I opened my eyes a crack to look at that maiden. I was the most blessed man in the world, hell, in two worlds. But I still felt a twinge of greed seeping into me.

I had Aphaera, so stunningly beautiful and perfect. I was about to take Nyphenah. And still, I was tempted to take this maiden. Not as a concubine, mind you, just a quick rut. To mark her, pump her full of my seed, and leave my mark on that tribe before I left.

I licked my lips at the idea and caressed Aphaera's figure.

I could have her, if I wanted. She was watching Aphaera clean me, her hands lathered in soap as she stroked my cock and gently cleansed my heavy, swollen sac. This was the longest I had gone without cumming since I first found Aphaera, my perfect slut, and she unleashed the man in me. She was massaging my balls, knowing full well how they ached.

The maiden was tanned and thin, wearing a simple brown dress to match her auburn hair. Her eyes were large, and she had a pleasantly dreamy expression as she watched me. She saw me drinking her in, and that made her smile, as well.

"Nyphenah is quite lucky, mighty Malchor. The stories of your arrival did not tell of your endowment," the maiden said.

"Would people have believed it if they had?" I boasted.

Damn, I was getting cocky.

I'd always kept a rein on my ego back on Earth. I worked out and kept myself in good shape, tried to avoid things lesser men lost themselves in. I never let it get out of control.

But with Aphaera emboldening and unleashing me, it felt silly to hold it back anymore. Instead, I just eyed that maiden, pondering whether she was worth the rut.

I'd started to think to myself: it'd be best to save my seed for the chieftain's daughter. But I remembered what Aphaera had said to me upon that altar: that any woman who laid with me even once would bear my child.

Was it true? I hadn't had a chance to prove it yet. Aphaera seemed certain that she was carrying my child already, but it was too soon to tell.

"Come closer," I beckoned the maiden with a wave of my hand.

She moved forward, tilting her head at me.

"What is it?" she asked, trying to maintain her gaze into my eyes, but it kept dipping down. She was memorizing every inch of my tanned, wet flesh as Aphaera cleaned the grime from it. Aphaera looked at me as well, questioning.

Part of me wanted to consult with Aphaera first, to see what she thought. Was I risking violating some taboo? Ruining the whole deal? But at that point, having beaten a horrible monster, saved a tribe, won the girl, and been tended to so dotingly… I felt like I was already the King of Kings.

"Before I'm fully cleaned and prepared for the ceremony, I will grant you a special offer," I said, as my cock achingly throbbed in Aphaera's dainty hands. I looked at the maiden, my eyes deep and serious. I didn't say the words, but I stared at her knowingly.

Aphaera's mouth opened, her brows furrowed, and I could sense her disapproval. But she was my girl, and she knew better than to question me.

The maiden stiffened, mulling my words over. I knew she wasn't going to resist, though, and it only took a second before she was stepping toward me again.

"I'm at your disposal, of course," she said, glancing over her shoulder.

The rest of the tribe was hard at work preparing for the ceremony and feast, out of sight, leaving just the three of us in the golden light of the late afternoon.

"First, what is your name?" I asked her. I let my eyes roam over her, undressing her as I licked my lips. She was pretty; not the stunning looker that Nyphenah was, nor did she possess the perfect beauty of Aphaera. But back home she'd easily be a stunning hottie. Well worth sticking your dick in.

"Fiadh, lord," she answered, her fingers running through her long, brown hair. "Shall I disrobe for you?"

Aphaera's mouth touched against my throat, kissing me there, letting me feel her wet body press against mine. I figured it was another test, too, ne that I'd have a more immediate answer to. Aphaera might be fine with me bedding allies that would strengthen us as we followed this plan she set in motion. But I wanted to see how jealous she'd get when I made her watch me fill a commoner with my seed.

I nodded to Fiadh's words, putting my arm around Aphaera and holding her as my dick throbbed.

"My mission will take me far from here before long, Fiadh," I said, caressing Aphaera's side, then cupping her breast. "But I will leave you with a very special gift that will make you the envy of the rest of the tribe," I said, so full of myself I believed it entirely in that moment.

The chieftain would have probably had my head for

fucking some random woman before his daughter. Or not. He was a hard man to read, I didn't know their customs, and I wasn't really interested in thinking it through.

Fiadh smiled as she let her dress fall from her shoulders, revealing her lithe, tanned body and that tiny pussy between her thighs. Her breasts were small but perky with puffy little nipples that were begging to be sucked, and as she turned, I caught sight of her firm ass.

She began to enter the water as Aphaera shifted to my side, her hands still on my broad shoulders.

Both of the women were waiting for me to tell them what to do. For me to live out my fantasies, using their bodies as I pleased.

I admired Fiadh's body, my dick twitching with excitement. This would be the first woman I'd fucked since Aphaera. The first besides her that I'd knock up.

"Aphaera, take hold of my cock," I told her, then commanded, "Fiadh, come here and straddle me." I rested my free arm back on the rocks as I lounged, reclining back.

I felt like a god in that moment.

Even more so as Aphaera dutifully took my hard, throbbing shaft and wrapped her diligent hand around it. She watched as Fiadh approached, and soon, the brunette's hands were on my chest as she found her footing. She didn't seem to need any foreplay. Hell, she didn't even need me to touch her. The second she was straddling, Aphaera lifted my cock, positioning it just so to let my swollen crown touch against another woman's bare pussy. Even in the water, I can feel her special wetness, her arousal so rich. Fiadh's nipples were puffy, and Aphaera leaned in, licking one as she stared at me.

I didn't stop them. I wanted to see what they'd do.

Fiadh watched me, her head tilting, her button nose scrunching up as she bit her lower lip, and then I felt it: her sweet, tight pussy, pressing down on me. She was either a virgin or hadn't been with anyone even close to my size, because it was not an easy fit. Her cheeks flushed as she had to use more of her strength to get even just the head of my thick cock within her walls, and I gotta say... it was bliss.

I swear, I never could've even imagined something like this back in my old world. It would have been too out there to even be a turn on. A fantasy so fantastical, it had no root in reality. Not to mention the fact that I'd had no interest in knocking a girl up before, so that wasn't a fantasy I turned to either. But as Fiadh let out a little grunt and Aphaera's mouth took her breast and suckled her nipple, she was finally able to take another inch. It didn't seem she had the strength to fight her body's resistance much more than that, though, not without help, and Aphaera picked up on that.

"Do you want me to guide her?" Aphaera purred, looking at me as she licked that perky nip again.

Normally, I would've been more involved. I would've taken over. Probably got on top of the overwhelmed girl and fucked her like that. Or at least put my hands on her hips and guided her, controlled her pace and tempo, used my strength to squeeze my thick cock up into her.

But in that moment, I was savoring being a man-god, and letting these two beauties cater to me. So I just nodded in response to Aphaera's question, my eyes opening to narrow slits as I studied them both in the gleaming light of the holy spring.

"She wishes to bear my seed. But she hasn't the willpower to handle getting there all on her own," I remarked, my voice lower and rumblier. My dick twitched and throbbed because of those couple inches inside of Fiadh.

"Mmm... how does it feel, Fiadh?" I asked, moving one hand from Aphaera's body to cup Fiadh's perky little breast, to squeeze and fondle it for my own curiosity, rather than to tease or please her.

She was firm and perky, and she gazed into my eyes.

"You are... I feel..." she said, struggling for the words.

"You have only just the tip of him," Aphaera purred. "I can jerk him off into your fertile little cunt, but you deserve to have him ruin you for every other man. Tell him that you deserve it," Aphaera ordered, her tone growing darker and more menacing.

"I deserve it," Fiadh moaned. "I want it."

Aphaera's hand grasped me tighter, stroking my dick as the crown was still lodged inside Fiadh. She teased the two of us as she leaned in, taking Fiadh's nipple between her teeth and giving it a tug. Her pert tit snapped back into place as the maiden let out a cry of pain, and Aphaera's grin grew.

"Dirty little whore. You're stealing the Chieftain's daughter's promised seed," Aphaera growled as she let my cock go and grabbed the girl's hips. "The least you could do is take him to the hilt."

In that instant, in a surprising display of strength and skill, Aphaera pushed the girl down on my cock the rest of the way, making Fiadh scream out without reserve. She was split on my cock, her thin body bulging with the new intrusion as the head of my dick crashed against her inner barrier.

I felt great satisfaction, grinning as I watched Aphaera--who had at first disapproved--now taunting and teasing and escalating the situation. I chuckled lowly, in between moans, while my thick cock throbbed and swelled inside Fiadh's tight little pussy.

I squeezed her breast, probably too harshly, and flicked my thumb over her nipple.

"These will get nice and big once you're swollen with my child," I said, my breathing heavier. "But you won't get there if you don't start riding my cock," I taunted her, my cock spurting pre inside that pretty thing.

I licked my lips and watched, relinquishing Fiadh's tit to instead caress Aphaera's cheek. My sweet girl. I had fallen for her so damn hard, and I didn't even know it. I think that was part of why I tested her: to make sure it wasn't all a game. To reassure myself that no, she was mine. She was never going to push aside her desire for me, no matter what. No matter how I behaved.

"Ride me, little whore. Steal Nyphenah's seed," I said with a grin.

It was only with Aphaera's help that she was able to. It wasn't that Fiadh regretted seducing me. I was just too much man for her, and she needed some help. So Aphaera pulled her up and almost off of me, then pushed her back down, loosening and slicking up her pussy walls so that she could pump faster. The water lapped around me with each thrust, and I watched her face as it contorted between pain and pleasure.

"You're so lucky," Aphaera taunted her. "This dick was meant for queens and goddesses, not the likes of you."

She leaned in, taking that nipple in her mouth again, sucking it hard and not relinquishing it this time. She had enough control over the maiden's body by now, and the harder Aphaera sucked, the more Fiadh's pussy quivered around me.

"I think she likes it," I said, reaching out and grabbing her other tit. I took her nipple between my thumb and forefinger my hands and tweaked it. Another quiver went through Fiadh's cunny, and I grinned.

Aphaera was right, I knew it then: that my cock was intended for fucking and impregnating queens and goddesses. But it was I who decided where it went. If I wanted to seed every maiden between here and wherever the fuck else in this harsh world? Then I would. I'd leave a trail of pregnant women behind me, I decided in that moment, grinning and moaning as my dick was serviced.

"A shame you aren't a perfect woman like my sweet Aphaera here," I said with a wistful sigh, my other hand coming up to caress Aphaera's hair. "Mm, then you might've been able to come with us. But it's more than you could've hoped for to be able to ride my dick just once, isn't it?" I asked Fiadh, staring at her and enjoying the sight of her pumping up and down my dick with Aphaera's help.

"Oh yes! Yes, my lord! This is the greatest blessing," she cried out, and I knew she meant it. There was no way she could fake how her pussy tightened around me, or how she started to leech control from Aphaera, pumping her little hips of her own volition now that she was stretched out enough to accommodate my huge dick.

I'd started that session with an ego the size of the Pacific Ocean. And the longer it went on... I swear, I had to have hit some new record.

But I lay back and enjoyed it all, moaning and groaning as my dick was ridden. I did nothing to help her or give her any pleasure beside allowing her to feel my huge cock splitting her open. I reached for my Aphaera, putting my arm around her and pulling her back to my side.

"Come here," I rumbled, kissing her deeply, passionately.

As crude and egotistical of a brute as I'd become, I still had a special place for my Aphaera. I caressed her side, lavished affection upon her as Fiadh did the work of pumping my cock up and down in her tight little pussy.

Aphaera's arms went around me, her nipple piercings pressed into my tight skin as she kissed up my throat.

"She will be addicted to you now," she whispered in my ear. "Once you cum in her, you will sow more than your seed in her," she said, licking along the cusp of my ear.

"Even your pre-cum is weakening her to your charms, especially these people with no defense against magic. Tell her to do something," Aphaera suggested.

I was fascinated by this new information. And while part of me should've been more dubious (was it just superstition on her part?) I believed it wholly in that moment, without a flicker of doubt.

"Say you're my obedient little cock sleeve," I told Fiadh,

then decided to up the ante a bit. "And slap yourself in the face," I added, looking between the two women.

Her pussy squeezed my dick as her mouth gaped open, and for a second I didn't think she was going to do it. But her little squeeze released a bit more of my cum, and suddenly, the words were spilling from her lips.

"I'm your obedient little cock sleeve," she moaned, before filling the air with the loud crack of her palm meeting her cheek.

And then, she came.

I wouldn't have believed it either, but her pussy gushed honey all over me as she obeyed my command, and Aphaera laughed with amusement.

"The chieftain's daughter will be your willing slave after a few doses," she whispered in my ear. "She will do or say anything. I wanted it to be a surprise for tonight, but you had to ruin it by opening a present early. The longer you go without cumming, the stronger it gets."

My eyes widened as I watched Fiadh become a slave to her desire for me, addicted to my seed, before I'd even properly blown my load inside her. A grin crossed my face, wide and arrogant. I kissed Aphaera again and moaned aloud.

"Do you have anything you'd like to put little Fiadh up to, my sweet?" I asked Aphaera in a low growl, caressing her hair and back. "Before I blow my load and seal her fate forever," I added. I licked my lip as I felt the tingles of approaching climax but held them at bay… for now.

Aphaera mulled that over, leaning in toward Fiadh, tongue flicking over her skin as she thought. Fiadh shuddered with delight, her orgasm having made her quite sensitive, before Aphaera looked at me.

"I think she's had too much of your dick, as is. She's not worthy of it. But I won't deny you the pleasure of her tight embrace," Aphaera said pleasantly. "I think she should make it tighter for you by putting two of her fingers in her ass."

I grinned at that suggestion, and looked back to Fiadh.

"Shove two of your fingers up your ass and keep them there until I'm done unloading," I commanded her. "Actually, on second thought… make it three. Force them in there," I added in a rough voice. "I'm about to blow my load and I want you to make it as good for me as you can."

I grinned at Aphaera, pulling her to me with my powerful arm, kissing her again and murmuring into her ear.

"We'll have plenty of time to get the Chieftain's daughter hooked on my seed. Don't worry," I assured her with a caress.

Fiadh stared at me, looking like she wanted to protest, but it was out of her control. She reached behind me, grabbed the oil she'd brought and squirted a copious amount into her hand. She watched me the entire time as she coated her fingers in it, then brought her hand around the tight swell of her ass.

The oil helped, as she started to work her fingers up inside of her, but this was clearly something she'd never done before. Hell, it was something I'd never done before either, and the sensation was intense. I could feel her nudge her fingers in through that tight ring, then further up. First one, then another, her body fighting her as it had fought me.

Aphaera grabbed Fiadh's nipple between her nails and tugged it again.

"Worthless slut," she growled before lunging in, sucking hard on her tit as Fiadh finally managed to fit the tip of her third finger.

I could barely move with her new, tighter clench, but I could feel her ministrations from inside, which were a delight of their own.

My cum made women my willing slaves.

How about that?

That realization only fueled my arrogance, which in turn fueled my pleasure. I shut my eyes and leaned back against the smooth stones, letting the sensations wash over me, and held nothing back.

I moaned and grunted, my dick swelling thickly as Fiadh struggled to ride me. At last, as Aphaera taunted the girl, teased her, and slipped her soft hand down to cup my balls, egging on my release…

I came. I blew my thick load of virile seed into that tight young tribal woman, flooding her fertile womb as my cock shot off stream after stream of my rich cum. It was intense, and if I hadn't been having mind-blowing sex with Aphaera every day since I met her, I'd have said it was the best orgasm of my life.

She screamed so loudly that I knew people must have heard, but I didn't care. She was going to milk me of every drop, with Aphaera helping my seed along.

The crown of my dick pressed against her womb, and she held herself there, letting me unload into her so deeply. She knew the risks, she knew what she was doing, and still she wanted it. Her body was writhing as Aphaera nipped and tugged at her teat, making it even puffier, while Fiadh's cunny drained me dry.

It was blissful and marvelous. I'd never see this woman again, but she'd not only bear my child, but forever carry the mark of having been mine for a fleeting moment. As the three of us wound down, every last tingle of pleasure extracted from my dick, I had Aphaera pull the woman off me.

"Take care of my child," I told her, knowing she was now loaded with my addictive cum. "And tell everyone you meet of my greatness, of how I will save everyone, and be the new King of all," I said with a grin, before letting the two women resume cleaning and preparing me.

Of course, I was so drunk on my own ego, I was totally unprepared for everything to go completely wrong. My biggest disaster yet.

CHAPTER ELEVEN

Before I even had a chance to feel a twinge of guilt about acting like an egotistical jerk, it became apparent that things weren't going to go according to plan. As the two women were ceremonially anointing me in oils, my body glistening, their soft, dainty hands caressing every bulge of muscle, every inch of my flesh… we heard cries coming from the camp. It didn't strike us as particularly odd right away; after all, a celebration was planned.

They must've been getting an early start to the celebration, we reasoned, none of us particularly wanting to rush our own part in things.

But before long, the cries became more… alarmed. I decided it was too much to ignore.

"Stand back, ladies," I said. I stepped toward my spear, picking it out of the ground and advancing. As I pulled back the thick bush just around the corner, someone came rushing from around it.

I very nearly stabbed him, until he fell down panting and wounded. I could see by his garb that he was with the tribe.

I didn't even have time to ask him what was wrong before a horse bearing a rider came charging toward him, lance at the ready to run him through. Reacting instantly, I lifted my own spear and deflected the rider's lance.

But saving that one man's life had brought attention to me. The rider veered back, pivoting his horse just as I saw what was happening in the distance: the tribe's camp was being raided by horseback riders. And these didn't look like the horrible, scraggly little fellows I'd beaten before. They seemed to have all their arms and eyes, riding dressed in black silk, with bronze armor over top.

It was utter chaos. The tribe clearly wasn't expecting this attack in the midst of their celebration. And just as the rider next to me was wheeling about to redouble his attack, another was approaching. I quickly jumped over the prone man and stabbed my spear up into the rider, making him scream as my stainless-steel cut through his armor.

The maiden ran. Her lithe legs pumped so fast as she took off into the distance to go protect the fruit I'd planted within her, but Aphaera was grabbing her bow, notching an arrow, readying herself to defend me.

Her arrow sang as it shot through the air, finding its mark in the distant rider's horse's leg, making it stagger forward as it whined in pain. The rider was doomed before he even got to me. As his horse wobbled and staggered, his balance thrown off, I managed to finish him off with a deft stab of my spear, sending him reeling back off his horse and to the ground with a thud.

"C'mon!" I said, gripping my spear with both hands as I advanced into the camp.

I was almost completely naked, wading into the fight without a thought for my own safety. I could see that the tribe was trying to get its defense in order, some of them racing for their weapons in the guards' yurt. But two riders blocked their way.

That was where I was needed most, I decided, ignoring the other fights waging around me. I ran in, ducked down to avoid the club swing from a passing horse, then charged up to the riders blocking the storage yurt.

"AAHHHH!" I yelled in a charge, gathering the attention of the riders. But horses are unwieldy things to turn, and he couldn't do it in time. Not before I had charged up and stabbed my spear into him, ending another of these invaders.

Aphaera stayed back in the darkness, trying to keep me safe as I fought. But a buxom beauty like her, naked and glistening, would draw attention if she wasn't careful. She hadn't wasted a second of a thought to grab her clothes before rushing off to protect me, and once I was inside, I knew she'd cover my rear.

As the other rider turned around and charged at me, one of her arrows sank into his armor. But the bone we'd carved her arrows with wasn't sharp enough to pierce his metal scale mail, it just wounded him. And he was still coming at me.

I roared and the two of us did battle. I hopped to one side to avoid a jab of his lance, then he deflected a jab of my spear. It was a tough fight. He had the advantage of height from atop his horse and he wasn't like the weak, wounded, emaciated men I'd battled with before. He was hale, hearty, and wearing actual armor, carrying an actual weapon.

But when the tribesmen began to dash around behind him, his attention suddenly became divided, and I found my opening. I jabbed my spear right into his stomach, and he cried out in pain. More than that, he gripped my spear to try and stop me from pushing it in deeper.

The bigger problem for me was that his grip also stopped me from hauling my weapon back out quickly, and just then, I saw another rider charging up on me.

For the first time, I felt a genuine twinge of fear.

But at the last moment, Aphaera came to the rescue. Her arrow struck true. No need to worry about piercing armor when it went right through the man's eye, sending him toppling back off his horse.

I grinned again, feeling the rush of triumph as I found another fight to join. Very soon the tribesmen were armed and at my back, helping take on the horseback riders. We started meeting up with some of the perimeter guards who had been overwhelmed but were now getting back into the fight seriously.

Just as things were starting to look good again, I saw him: a man atop a giant black steed, garbed in black and bronze, much the same as the others. Except his helm was like a terrible crown.

He was clearly the leader of the group, and wherever he went, death followed.

I knew I had to end him, that once I did, this whole raid would fall apart. I'd be the hero all over again.

But as I began to sprint toward him, more riders closed in, ringing their leader. I was forced to reel back to avoid their lances, and their numbers only increased, as more of them clashed into us from the side, taking the attention of the guards.

I was pinned and made useless. While Aphaera's arrows had helped, the two of us weren't enough to end their threat quickly.

So I had to watch--in flickering glances--as that black knight captured my concubine-to-be. Nyphenah.

The poor young thing was dressed so beautifully, her stunningly full-figured body on display as she was bound at the wrists and ankles and thrown over the back of his horse. And I swear our eyes met, hers and mine, for just a moment.

I ran and slid beneath a horse to try and get to her. But the leader looked at me as he began to reel around, letting forth a sharp, unearthly whistle that rallied his men.

I was hellbent on stopping him, though, and pumped my powerful legs. But just as I was getting close--oh so very, very close--more riders swept in, and I was knocked back onto my ass like a fool.

They were in retreat, but that alone wasn't going to save me. I looked up and saw one of the riders charging in, ready to split me open with his lance. I wouldn't be able to react in time, I knew. This was likely going to be it for me.

But from the protection of the shrubs, another arrow soared from Aphaera's bow and caught this man under his shoulder, finding a spot in the armpit his armor didn't cover. He dropped his lance and charged on in pain, and I was left in the chaotic camp.

Everything had gone to shit so quickly. I was feeling so fucking good, like I was on top of the world. The dark rider had humiliated me, weakened my ally, and stolen my concubine. I would not allow that to stand!

I ran, doing all the damage I could to their retreating numbers, but they were on horseback and they were smart. They had come to the camp with a plan that they executed and lost relatively few of their force along the way.

I wasn't going to let them embarrass me like that, but as I pushed my spear through another enemy, the distance between the raiders and me grew. Nyphenah's scream cut through the air before it, too, faded into the night.

The rest of the night was something of a blur as the heat of failure and shame burned through me. But in truth, the tribesfolk didn't blame me. In fact, they seemed to see me as their savior. And while they mourned the loss of some of their own, they thanked me as I walked past them back into camp, some even kneeling to me in reverence.

But I could see the chieftain was in a rage himself, but he saw his people's attitude toward me, and kept it in check.

"Tell me, what are you going to do about my missing daughter?" he glowered at me through gritted teeth and barely-suppressed rage.

I stood there, trying not to let that feeling of defeat show in how I stood or spoke. I looked at the chieftain, narrowing my eyes.

"I am going to take my woman back," I said in a low growl. "And nobody is going to stop me."

My angry, stubborn declaration seemed to raise the spirits of some of the tribe, as some smiles sprouted up. Aphaera came to my side, as the chieftain asked: "Who were these men? They were not like the Warlord-King's usual brutes."

"That's because they're no brutes. They are his elite, the Black Marauders. We didn't stand a chance, not without planning," Aphaera said, her bare chest still heaving from battle as one of the women offered her a simple white robe. She accepted it, pulling it on over her head before she looked at me. "The man you saw was their general. A merciless man who spends his time hunting down enemies of Moloch."

I looked down at her, my sweet, loyal Aphaera. I was surprised by her insight and knowledge of this man and his forces, but then... maybe not so surprised. She was so wise and learned. She'd pushed me further than I'd ever dared dream in such a short time.

"Then this must've been planned before we even arrived," I said, realizing finally that not everything was about me.

"So his goal was always to take my Nyphenah?!" the chieftain roared, slamming his fists on his ceremonial seat made of some kind of bone or shell.

"You have made yourself a powerful enemy of Moloch," Aphaera said. "You lead, you thrive without his presence. Should his people find out about you and your tribe, it would be chaos and rebellion," she said, but there was something else. Something she was hiding from the chieftain. He didn't seem to notice it, he was so consumed by his fury, but I sure did, and I was going to ask her about it in private.

"Then his goal must be to blackmail the chieftain into ending his rebellion," I said, clenching the spear in my hand tightly. I could see the chieftain reacting similarly, as our eyes met, full of rage and desire for vengeance.

"Do not fear," I said to the chieftain, "this injustice is mine as much as yours. I swore to you that we are like kin now, and I meant it."

I puffed out my broad chest. "I will go and reclaim your daughter, my bride. And I will make the Black Marauders regret ever setting hoof in your camp," I declared firmly, to some cheers and hollers from the tribespeople surrounding us.

The chieftain was bristling with rage, and words weren't coming easily to him. He nodded his head, then waved his hand.

"You must try to rest. I am sending word to the other camps to rally together. Because at dawn, we will be at war once more, to reclaim my daughter and defend our freedom," he declared with a booming voice that caused the tribe to cheer.

Aphaera put her hand on my arm, gently guiding me away toward the yurt that had been prepared as a matrimonial room for me. It was adorned with the finest bed and silks the tribe had, but it all felt tainted now. I felt the loss of my woman deep in my soul, and I ached to protect her from the dangerous man who took her.

I entered in with Aphaera, putting my spear to one side as I grappled with my failure to protect Nyphenah. But then my eyes trailed back to Aphaera, and I asked without hesitation, "What were you keeping back from the chieftain in there?"

She licked her lips, hesitating. Her golden hair was a spun mess around her face, her green eyes nearly glowing in the flickering light of the oil candles. But when she finally looked at me, her shoulders softened, and she relented.

"You must not be angry as I tell you what I've done. I have very good reasons," she said softly as she went to the bed, still looking up at me.

I hadn't expected the conversation to take such a turn. I knew she had her secrets about her background, but I never pried. I worried it might be a wound, and asking questions might slice it back open. So instead, I went with her to that bed, sat down, and put an arm around her to draw her close.

"Tell me," I bade her, my voice firm but low. "You can trust me with anything." Though that was perhaps not entirely true. I had fallen for her, and the way she made me feel so… unstoppable. But I was so full of myself and righteous rage, there were a lot of secrets probably best kept from me at that time.

"I am sure you've pieced together that Moloch is hunting me for a reason, and that my return to his Kingdom is important. He did not realize how… adept I am in battle. He had no reason to think of me as anything more than a woman. That is why the bounty hunters were on my trail, and maybe had partly to do with why that army attacked us," she began, covering all the things I'd already figured out on my own.

"But before I left, I tried to spread… hope. Or what passes for it, under his watchful eye. The hope of freedom, of something better."

The full picture was beginning to take form around me. The reason she knew of this tribe. How she knew what to negotiate with. The tales of their strengths and weaknesses. She'd known so much because they were her source of hope. She hadn't expected to find me. She expected to find *them*.

I wasn't upset at her, even then, for keeping that from me. I caressed her side, then pushed some stray strands of hair away from her face gingerly.

"I knew you had to be a very important woman in this world," I said to her, my voice low and rumbly. "Because you are very important to me, too."

I pressed my head to hers and kissed her forehead. "You have helped push me to new heights in so short a time, I can only imagine how important you must have been to him… as an 'entertainer'," I said, referencing our first meeting.

"He does not like losing people. Or the perception of losing people. He is controlling, overbearing, paranoid. He makes the lives of his people hell, even when they are obedient. But you are innocent of this, Malchor. You did not deserve to be pulled into this. But my finding you was fate."

It had struck me that the chieftain knew of my coming, just as she had, under that strange name she'd gifted me. I wondered what tales of Malchor had spread to the Warlord-King, and if he knew who I was. I doubted it, as communication was slower without those tiny, shiny beeping-machines that we all carried constantly back in the old world.

I squeezed her against me, holding her tightly in my strong arm as I mulled it all over. My journey to become a king was still fresh, new. Once word spread of me and my deeds, the heat would only get exponentially worse. But I didn't find that so daunting. At least, not as daunting as I should have.

"I will keep you from him," I swore to her, though she hadn't mentioned anything about that fear. "Until the very end, when we cast him down and end his terrible reign," I declared, kissing her once more. "I pledge it to you."

"Oh, Malchor," she breathed out, her body relaxing against mine. "You are better than I could have dreamed, but we still have so much to do before we can defeat him. His elite fight without honor, without mercy. They defile all who cross them without remorse. It is their greatest strength, and I hope to turn it into their greatest weakness, as well. But the future is still so muddled..."

I wrapped her up in my arms and held her, caressed her, kissed her. I knew she was pushing me toward a destiny I didn't much want to reach when we first set out. But the more I went down this road toward becoming a champion, a king? The more I wanted it. The more I wanted to please her by becoming everything she dreamt I was.

"I know we will get there," I said boldly. "I will conquer all those in our path, and you will provide the wisdom and cunning to let me see that path."

She stroked my cheek, the simple dress she was given rustling against my side.

"The people under him are unhappy, kept in check by fear. They will support him as long as they think he's the likely ruler. But if they believe there is another, someone just and fair, they will revolt. He keeps them weak, only allowing those in his elite army to train and fight. I learned in the shadows, though, and so did others. Weakening his reputation by taking out the general and ensuring the people hear about it will go far to securing your future."

I looked into her emerald eyes, their intoxicating glow. How I loved her, without even realizing how deeply in over my head I was. She was a true woman, in every sense of the word. And I was so eager to be her champion. Her protector. Her Malchor.

"Tomorrow we set out to try and find Nyphenah," I said, kissing her again. "We will need all the strength and cunning we can muster to do it, and set the stage for our eventual victory. But you believe in me, don't you?" I asked, wanting to hear her say it.

"There is no one else who can kill the Warlord-King except for you, Malchor. The people have been praying for you to reveal yourself for so long," she said, with all that earnestness and love rich in her voice. "You will prevail and breed a new dawn."

"I've already started… with you," I said, one of my large hands sliding from her hip to her stomach, placed over her womb, where I knew--felt it in my heart and loins--that my child was already taking shape inside her. I had fallen head over heels for this woman, and believed all she said.

I just didn't know what she was still holding back, and everything that path would entail.

CHAPTER TWELVE

Aphaera and I made love that night. Not the raunchy fucking like rabbits we'd been doing since we met, but tender lovemaking. I won't go into it any more than that here, because it was both special and a little painful, for reasons I haven't gotten to yet, to dwell on.

I never came in the end. I laid her out beneath me, I slid inside her and made her climax, but I held back my own.

"Let the tension simmer inside me to help build rage for the revenge we're going to take," I said, thinking about how I was going to use that frustration to fuel my attack on the Warlord-King's general.

We awoke the next morning to the sound of horns crying out, the whole tribe working busily. When we stepped out of the yurt, we could see that the tribe had gathered together its other camps, and now hundreds were amassed, if not more. Although, not all of them would be marching off to fight, because many were women or children.

"We should go speak with the chieftain," I said, before I saw him approaching us in his full battle garb of leather and chitin.

"We are nearly ready to set out. Our scouts have reported the area in which this general has led his Black Marauders," he said.

Aphaera's and my outfits had been returned to us at some point in the night, and they had repaired the damage sustained in the fight with that horrible mind-beast. They'd even added some extra armor to mine, in the form of what I later learned were chitin plates. Shells from giant bugs, I was told.

We were ready to fight, and to hear that the scouts were already giving reports took a weight off. It was nice not to have to do it all on my own, I had to admit.

"Is General Zarizh heading back to the Warlord-King's domain?" Aphaera asked. I knew she didn't think that was likely. Something about it had seemed off to her, but she wasn't able to really explain why.

"The scouts do not believe so," the chieftain said, running his hand through his hair in frustration. "There is a darkness gathering on the horizon, ash rising to the air. That is the direction they are heading."

Aphaera squeezed my hand.

"Toward the far mountains in the West?" she asked, and the chieftain responded in the affirmative.

She looked to the sky, doing some calculations in her mind that I could not fathom.

"There are thirteen days before the new moon, and it is a twelve-day journey on foot," she mused, deep in thought. "If they can delay us even a day, we will be too late."

I looked at her with a furrow of my brow.

"Too late for what?" I asked, confused and curious. "What are they planning?"

"A ritual. Blood binds your people," Aphaera said to the chieftain. "Your daughter's blood remains pure, and she is your direct descendant. A sacrifice under the blackest of nights would corrupt your bloodline, poison it. But it would also reach out to any that Nyphenah has touched. If the Warlord-King is not taking her as his own, then that's what I believe he would do. It would explain why she was taken captive. The only benefit, then, is that she will remain untouched. Unharmed. They would not risk the Warlord-King's wrath, not his elite."

I could see the look of extreme concern and fear on the chieftain's face, and I felt the urgency of the moment.

"Then it's not blackmail after all. He wishes to use dark sorcery to bend these people to his will, where the threat of violence failed?" I spoke up.

I was reminded of the cruel and petty men I knew back in my world who became bosses, or figures of authority, just so that they would have sway over other men, purely to abuse it. A certain special someone burned in my mind, and I knew that I had to get going to stop this.

"The tribe's forces will be ready to go in a few hours. But you," the chieftain said, looking at me. "You and a small band of our scouts could make time faster. Especially if you set out right away."

"I will do it," I said without hesitation. "I'll lead the scouts and we'll find your daughter, Chieftain. And we will do what's necessary to free her," I swore.

While there were no cheers this time, I could see the look of resolute certainty on those war-band members around us.

We didn't have the advantage of speed, but Aphaera hoped that they would not be in a rush, given the timeline. They could take their time, pillage as they went, and still make it for the new moon. Aphaera assured me that it would happen when the moon could not be seen. Perhaps it was the multiple suns or the size of the planet or whatever, but moon cycles took longer here, and I was grateful for that.

Even without mounts of our own, things progressed

quickly. A band of scouts rallied with us, and together we set out with supplies. The tribespeople couldn't spare much time, but they did bid us good fortune quickly before returning to their duties, preparing the bulk of their army for war.

It was only when the tribe was well behind us that I could look back and get a true idea for just how many of them there were. And more seemed to be arriving. If there had been thousands of them, I wouldn't be surprised.

Our band was small, numbering about a dozen, all told. But at the head were Aphaera and I to lead them. I could sense that they felt reassurance at our presence.

Their tracks weren't hard to follow in the dusty soil, and the first day of the journey went rather unremarkably. At night, we settled in once rest was required and made camp around a small area. We found a little enclosed rocky area, where it was safe to light a fire without being seen. There, one of the tribal scouts, a woman, showed me how to better bind my spear's pole n leather hide, to strengthen it and ensure my steel tip didn't ever slip free.

Aphaera went off to a corner of the camp, looking up at the sky. I knew of her strength in magic, her connection to some mystic force of this universe. I saw her perform a great ritual in that temple, and appreciated her understanding of what the Warlord-King was planning.

But this was the first time I saw her really pray.

She sat for so long and I watched from afar, foreign words coming to me on the wind when it picked up. When she finally returned, looking over the work I'd done on my spear, she was sullen.

"The Goddess is silent tonight. Her strength lies in the fullness of the moon, representing the fullness of pregnancy and life, and as it wanes, so does her voice," Aphaera explained to me quietly.

"She merely leaves this task to us because she knows it is

within our abilities," I reassured her, putting an arm around her again. "You will see, this will all go well. It will mark the first big strike against the Warlord-King and his armies. Word will spread, as you predicted, and we will be on our way towards final victory." I even believed my own bullshit in that moment.

Of course, it was much easier to believe it while I relaxed in a camp, looking up at the bright, starry sky and feeling the press of my hot concubine against my skin, rather than staring down the wrong end of a sword.

She nodded, though, because she believed my bullshit, too.

"You are right. And saving these people, letting them stand as a beacon of freedom and community... it will all be worth it, great Malchor. We are doing a good thing."

I smiled down at her, caressed her blonde hair that she'd carefully tied back again, and kissed her. She was a great source of comfort to me. Looking back, she made all my years of being the "lone wolf" feel silly and empty by comparison.

Sure, I could have been a success by the measure of my old world. I could dare to do things others wouldn't. I could accomplish all manner of feats. But what's a man without a woman at his side? To help him, guide him, to bear his children? A life without those things no longer held a shred of appeal to me. Not that my old achievements ever felt satisfying. At best, I felt some momentary thrill when I accomplished something great, dared to dive into some dangerous cave, or won a promotion. Only to be left with the hollow emptiness thereafter.

No, as grim as things were in that moment, I fell asleep holding my woman by my side, relishing the fact that while our lives were in danger, we were on a mission. A mission worth completing.

We didn't tarry long. We rested, and by morning--before

the sun had even risen--we were on our way again. But the tracks were harder to follow now since the wind was blowing the dusty earth around, hiding it for the Marauders. Our prospects seemed dark that day, since we were falling behind, with no sign of being able to catch up. And then...

It got a whole lot worse.

CHAPTER THIRTEEN

We entered into a valley, and felt some momentary excitement that the valley, protected from the wind, would preserve the tracks we were following. But we were soon greeted with a hideous sight.

One of the tribesmen was cut open, the gore of his body left as bait for wild beasts. He was dead, so there was no more suffering, but the buzzards that flew off at our approach wouldn't be the last to pick his remains.

Aphaera's arrow was notched and ready, her eyes wild with panic as she watched the body hit the ground with a sickening, wet *shlick*. He had been severed in two, his guts bleeding out and staining the rocks red.

We looked up to see two large silhouettes peering down on us from the crest of the hills on either side of the valley. They were big enough to be horses, but… something was off about them. Their black silhouettes were impossible to make out any clearer with the suns bright at their backs.

"Watch out!" I shouted. But before we could act, the creatures bounded down the hills like no horse could.

Once they reached us, I had my spear bared and ready to fight.

I wasn't, however, prepared for the strange, monstrous creatures that approached us. They were bigger than horses, but looked like some combination of lizards and bugs. They walked on six legs, with scaly, lizard-like hides between the chitinous plates that protected their bodies and limbs.

They had fanged maws, and hissed at us as they stood looming over the corpse, clearly drawn by the smell of that fresh meat, same as the buzzards.

"We must go!" shouted one of the tribesmen. "These are ashki! Sacred beasts, vicious and able to rend a man with their claws."

"But it is a sin to kill one," explained a scout.

But I knew that if we backed off, we would only lose more time as we found a way around the valley.

"We can't spare the time," I growled, advancing toward the two beasts.

Aphaera looked torn between respecting the customs of the tribe and her need to protect me and help me on my journey. She looked to the scout master.

"We will not let you kill a sacred beast. But Malchor will protect us on our path!" she shouted before bounding backward to find a clear shot.

I approached, brazen and full of myself, as if these two giant lizard-beasts would quiver before me. But then, a strange thing began to happen: I felt the cold chill of that black gemstone in my leather pocket. Its coolness was so jarring when all the world felt hot.

But as the lizard-beasts hissed and bared their fangs at us, they seemed to respond to that icy chill...

And instead of attacking, they ducked down, their forked tongues licking the air as they seemed to bow their heads in reverence. I was taken aback, but not as much as the tribespeople who were staring wide-eyed in absolute shock.

Aphaera didn't see it until at last she turned around, bow at the ready, and froze in stunned silence.

I didn't understand the magic in that gem when I'd taken it as a prize from that monster. But I had felt it call to me, that there was a purpose behind it.

It seemed like I'd just found that purpose, and never before had I felt my destiny so intertwined with fate as I did in that moment. Aphaera returned to my side much more slowly than she had left it, as though in a trance, and she stayed several feet behind me. She was being cautious, which was wise given that a man was still bleeding out a few feet from us.

But I carefully approached those sacred beasts, hideous and giant, but beautiful in a strange, exotic way. As I shifted my spear to one hand, then reached out slowly... I saw the creature flicker its eye-membrane, then give a low hiss.

I dared--foolishly--to reach out and pet its head. Its scales were smooth to the touch, and it seemed to crave the heat of my body. I caressed its head for a while, then got an idea.

"Wait," I told Aphaera as I moved around to the side of that giant creature with its dagger-length claws. I very brazenly began to mount it, swinging my strong leg up over its back as it lay down, as if waiting for me to do that very thing.

I looked out over the tribe as I sat atop their sacred beast, feeling its cool body between my thighs. One by one, they began to kneel, a few of them crying out in amazement. These people whom the gods had forsaken were witnessing a miracle, and once more, it was because of me.

Because of Malchor the great.

Aphaera stepped toward the animal, but she was much slower. She was not Malchor, and didn't want to take unnecessary chances, but they did not lunge for her either. They seemed calmed by my presence somehow. Or the presence of the gem. Either way, as I looked out at our scouting party, I felt triumphant. If I could use the beast as a steed, we could quickly gain on the army, snuffing them out before they even neared the ritual site.

I had an idea and we had to test it out. I reached down to Aphaera to take her hand. The lizard-beast--the ashki--didn't raise a fuss. It let me haul her up on top of the beast with me, nestling her behind me. The two of us held onto ridged flares of its chitinous shell for support.

I looked out at the awestruck tribespeople, and gestured to the other beast. It would be able to hold three of them, at least… if they allowed it.

Most of the tribespeople looked too horrified to even consider it, but a few stepped forward, some more excitedly than others. They approached the beast. It hissed more aggressively than it had at me, but it simmered back down when I looked at it.

And soon, the scouts were mounting it, too. Not everyone was able to fit atop though, and I looked at those remaining.

"We're going on ahead," I said. The ashki seemed to understand my will. It moved where and when I wanted it to, and the other one did the same, transporting the scouts. "You head back, inform the tribe of what's happened. Tell them of this portent, and that the Marauders seek to waylay and slow us at every turn."

They were enthralled by me, by the miracle I had just performed, and even those too frightened to fly the ashki were excited to return to the tribe with this news. They wasted no time as they turned back in the direction we'd come, their steps energized as they left the valley.

There was only one that lingered, and it was just for a moment, to take the items from his fallen comrade. I assumed he meant to return them to his family. They had no god to pray to, no last rites, but every person mourns in their own way. Once he was able to get the last of his usable worldly possessions, he too was off, sprinting to catch up to the others.

Aphaera's arms tightened around my waist and excitement vibrated through her body.

I turned my head as I guided the ashki in the right direction, speaking just for Aphaera.

"You made the right bet when you hitched yourself to my fate," I told her, so confident even after the previous day's disaster. I started the beasts off at a moderate pace, which caused us all to lurch, and one of the scouts nearly fell off his mount.

They were a smoother ride than a horse, for the lizard-creature's six legs moved almost independently, keeping its body, and thereby us, at an even point. There was no bucking around like with one of those damned horses.

Once we became used to our new transport, it felt like an extension of our own bodies, and it made for a gentle ride. I felt such a connection with them, as if our minds were linked, and I wondered if that was the gem's doing or just mine. After all, the gem had been possessed by a mind-bending creature, but I was nearly immune to it. Still, I wasn't willing to take a risk and toss the gem aside, and I made sure to secure it to myself more tightly as we made our way through the rocky terrain.

Nobody needed to know about my suspicions regarding the gem. It would only dampen their enthusiasm and spirits, and we had a big fight ahead. At least, that's what I told myself. In honesty, the allure of being seen as a holy figure of might and prowess was intoxicating. It added to the swell of my pride as Aphaera clung to me, holding on tight.

"We're making much better time now," I declared, and in truth we were. The ashki managed to carry us at over double our previous speed, and I had a feeling we were outpacing the Marauders' horses too. At that point it was only a question of endurance: could they keep it up? We didn't know yet. But everyone put their faith in me that they would, and we carried on.

It was getting darker, clouds beginning to blot out the larger sun. It cooled the air a little, and I didn't think much of it. We were leaving behind desert terrain and entering the mountains, and honestly, I was getting excited at the prospect it might rain. Maybe a little bit of it was because I thought I'd look badass as the water whipped through my hair, glistening on my body and washing away the blood of my enemies.

My dreams were getting more outlandish by the day.

My nightmares, though, were getting more terrifying by the hour.

CHAPTER FOURTEEN

I thought it was snow, at first. The little white flakes softly fell to the ground, beginning to blanket the land ahead of us. It wasn't until I felt it on my arm that I realized something wasn't right. Firstly, it was still too hot for snow. Secondly... it was not a snowflake.

"Ash," Aphaera said, shifting behind me.

The sky had been covered in what I thought were clouds, but they weren't made of water. They were smoke and ash, just up too high for me to really appreciate it. I saw it wafting from over the horizon toward where we were headed, but the mountain ridge ahead of us blocked my view of the volcano that Aphaera said was the location of the ritual.

"I think I would've preferred snow," I said, as we carried on.

The darkening skies were an ill omen, but whenever I found the scouts' courage flagging, they turned to me and I gave them a confident--well, cocky--smile, and we carried on with renewed spirits.

There were few other traps left by the Marauders, some rubble I was told wasn't there last time they traversed the valley, for instance. But nothing our ashki couldn't get over or around with relative ease.

A couple days passed, and the great beasts proved resilient: riding all day, then resting and devouring whatever meat or plant matter they could get their maws on in the evening. They were ravenous creatures that ate heartily of whatever was available. But hey, I could relate.

We were hot on the trail of the Marauders; we knew this because their tracks were suddenly clear again. They couldn't have been more than a few hours ahead of us. But then things took a severe turn for the worse.

The ash that had been falling was getting heavier. And the air was both cooler from the lack of sun and teeming with energy that gave it a feeling of unpleasant warmth. The winds began to pick up, and the ash was cutting through us as the grey clouds from the volcano turned darker until, even at the midpoint of day with two suns overhead, the sky was nearly black.

I finally got to see the volcano clearly, as we emerged from the valley and canyons beyond. And while I'd been curious about it, I wasn't prepared for just how ominous it looked.

It wasn't like the volcanoes back home. It was like a jagged hook coming out of razor-blade mountains. Snow capped the mountains above, but the one we were approaching had only the blanket of ash, as a seemingly endless stream of black ash spewed out of the top.

"It's getting hard to breathe," I said, coughing as the air grew heavier.

Aphaera offered me a slip of fabric, and I held it over my nose, trying to clear my lungs. But the ash was also cutting into my face and eyes, and while it seemed so delicate, it traveled at a dangerous speed. It began to make my eyes water and burn, and Aphaera ducked behind my back to shield herself from the worst of it.

"We should find shelter until the storm passes," she called out to me.

I was loath to give up on the chase when we were so very, very close. But one look at the other scouts convinced me we had to do it. They were barely holding on. And even the ashki themselves seemed daunted by the ash storm brewing.

"Let's find some shelter, a cave… anything!" I called to them, and we began to keep our eyes out not for the Marauders, but some place to wait out the storm.

It was not a moment too soon that we began, because the storm only got worse. In the distance, we saw the explosion of red lightning crackling through the ash storm. It was like nothing I'd seen back on Earth: terrible electrical spikes seemed to shoot both down *and up* through the ash clouds, forming explosive balls of fiery heat and energy at points.

It was so loud and terrifying, when added to the wind, I couldn't even hear Aphaera shouting to me as she clung to my back. We lost sight of the scouts, but I had a feeling the other ashki was still alive out there… somewhere.

Time seemed to stand still as we searched, moving as if we were in a vat of molasses. It was getting so hard to fight the strength of the wind. Several times we were blown back, the ashki's nimble footing faltering and jerking Aphaera and I backward.

The black sky turned to a sickening purple color, like a fresh bruise, in the wake of the lightning ball. The sound was like thousands of fireworks all going off at once, the crackling heat swirling at the mouth of the volcano. It was the only light cast upon the world, but it was too blinding, too bright, and it made it even harder to spot shelter.

But then, finally, I spotted something: a place without ash. A crevice in the hills, I thought, and I tried to guide the ashki in that direction. It was agonizingly slow going, and as we neared, I realized that it was too tight of a confine, even for Aphaera, and disappointment gripped my chest.

There was another flash of light, and green, putrid gases erupting from the lightning coalesced in the sky above us. A few seconds later, I heard a loud scream that was immediately drowned out by the thunder that followed. It boomed through my body, vibrating my organs, making me feel like I had when I first stepped through that portal.

We did our best to search out the source of that scream, and it led us to a cave opening, the strangest I'd seen so far.

Its mouth was round, the stones within it smooth. The stone was all black, and I realized it must've been a tunnel formed by lava long ago. Like an empty vein of the world.

It looked ominous, but we had no choice.

"Come on," I said as I dismounted from the ashki and pet its head again. I led the way, weapon at the ready--not that I could see anything--as we entered the dark tunnel.

The wind began to die down behind us, but it was so dark ahead. The blackness of the sky outside was amplified by the cave's black walls.

Inside, we heard two distinct sorts of sounds: the howling of the wind and rumbling thunder that followed those horrible strikes of volcanic lightning, which had gone from red to some shade of purple mixed with yellow, and the cave sounds. Much quieter, the cave had a strange echoing effect that carried every little noise great distances down its tube-like tunnels. So when we heard something that sounded like wet breathing, we had no idea where it was coming from.

I was somewhat used to it; the way caves play tricks on a man's mind. I had done some spelunking into the deep rocks and stones and learned what it meant to have a sound envelope you, unable to place its source.

I looked to our ashki, and with a tender pet to its smooth but scaly head, I bade it to wait in the shelter near the entrance before we moved onward. It bowed its head to me again and curled up, with its gaze moving back toward the entrance.

"Corgash will stay here. Protect us from any attack on our rear," I said, having named the beast in my head on the journey, but only then saying it out loud for the first time.

I took Aphaera's hand. For the first time since I'd met her, outside of life-or-death situations, she seemed scared. Her footsteps were reluctant as I guided us into the lava tube. We had some of these where I was from, but exploring them was still on my bucket list, so I felt excited. That rush, that thrill of exploration filled me.

I always felt called back to caves. I didn't know why. Even after my spelunking gone awry ended me up in this place, I never felt as afraid of caves as would have been wise.

I should have listened, when Aphaera said that this place was alive.

CHAPTER FIFTEEN

Maps and climbing equipment, lights, scuba gear... We had none of it, barring my climbing pick, and as we wandered along the worn-down walls of the solid rock, doubts began to creep into my mind. Aphaera was jumpy, constantly jerking around, and I wasn't sure if it was her mind playing tricks on her or if she was just seeing something I wasn't.

But some part of me, in the lizard part of my brain, swore it sensed something off. My hair was standing on end as we followed the meanders. The path widened to a gaping maw and then tapered off to just the right size for a man.

How could that be?

It was so perfect, so engineered, it seemed hard to believe that it was nature at work. That the natural world had carved this gift into the earth, just for me to explore.

But the deeper we went, the more it felt like we were indeed inside something living: something far bigger than us that might not even notice our intrusion. I prayed it wouldn't.

There were moments of perfect stillness interspersed with pockets of warm air pushing past us. As if they weren't veins, but an air passageway channeling currents around us. It was warm as it pushed against our faces, but somewhat cooler as it was sucked past our backs. And all around us, sounds seemed... off.

Aphaera was right beside me, yet sometimes I couldn't hear her at all. All the while, there was this dripping sound, even though we saw no water.

As we turned a corner we found ourselves immersed in absolute darkness. The pitch black draped around us like an all-encompassing blanket.

"Wait," I said, gripping her hand to keep her close. I felt her curl into my bicep and forearm for comfort.

But no amount of waiting helped our eyes adjust. There was no light, no matter how minuscule, to power our sight. It wasn't a cloudy night; it was the eternal darkness of a cave.

We tried to turn around and go right back to where we were around the corner. But somehow... it wasn't there. We were unable to find the trail that had been right behind us! The task of even finding the cave wall that was but a foot away now seemed herculean.

And then, after some wandering, we stopped and heard ghastly sounds. Like the gnashing of teeth on something wet. It sent a chill up my spine.

Luckily, I still had a flashlight. I'd not busted it out since I met Aphaera, for fear of wasting its battery. That thing was irreplaceable here, after all. But I reached for it at my waist, pulling it out and flipping the switch...

Light bathed the black-stone chamber of the lava tube, and we saw before us the crouched figure of a Black Marauder, hunched over a bloody form, feasting on it like he was some wild, carnivorous beast.

Aphaera's eyes took a moment to adjust in her surprise, having no warning -- or understanding -- of what a powerful portable light I carried. Maybe it seemed like magic to her, and she stared toward the thing I held, rather than the source of horror before us. It was only when she saw my face that she turned and swallowed a gasp, as her trembling hands grabbed for her bow.

He was within a cracked indentation in the stone, like the place where the gaseous lava had pooled, eating through the rock. It had formed a dome-like bubble, then, as it cooled, it shrank, pulling away from the stone walls and creating a sense of misshapen wrongness to the cave.

Why, of all the places in this cave, did the Marauder bring his prey there?

I didn't have the time to ponder it. I just sprang into action.

But as I rushed in to get the drop on him, I saw that what he was eating was no game meat. It was a human, one of the tribespeople, their insides ripped out, their head twitching, as their entrails were gnashed upon. It was such a gory sight it made me pause in horror, my mind reeling.

And in that moment, I lost the initiative. The ghostly white face of the Marauder, only visible below the gleaming metal mask that covered the upper portion of his face, turned to look over its shoulder at me, with sharp, bloody teeth. It screamed, and from out of the shadows, beyond where my light reached, another Marauder sprang like a panther.

I was knocked to the ground, the flashlight clattering away as I attempted to roll with the strike and flip my attacker over. With a kick I sent him flying against the jagged rock walls on his way, but now the only light we had was pointed in a series of random directions as it rolled around the uneven floor of the lava chamber.

Worse still, Aphaera, the steady partner I'd had at my side for so long, was shaking. Her first arrow went wide, ricocheting off the tunnel wall before falling to the floor like a dud. She was terrified, and that fear combined with the horrors ahead of us and the lack of ready light was holding her back. I had to buy us time while she got control of her nerves, but these guys were tough.

Inhumanly tough.

The one who'd been feasting on a living human had turned to join the fray. But he was going for Aphaera, and I couldn't let that happen. She was mine, and I wouldn't let anyone do a thing to her.

I sprang up and went for my machete, rushing to get between her and the cannibal monster. But before I could reach her, I felt sharp claws rake over my back, as the one I'd sent careening into the walls had already rebounded, and was using his metal gauntlets as a weapon.

I grunted in pain and struck back at him with an elbow, impacting his face. But he hardly seemed to budge from the hit, which I didn't understand. These fuckers had gone down the same as any man back at the tribal camp, when I'd helped the defense. Now they seemed to be made of solid stone.

Regardless, I pressed on, hammering my elbow into the man's face as I saw my dear Aphaera cowering back in the flickering light, trying to avoid the attacks of the bloody fiend. I couldn't take it anymore; I pursued the other one, even as the first one clawed at my back.

It was a rough moment, but I pounded into the Marauder attacking Aphaera with my body's full physical force, sending him crashing into the wall. He coughed up blood on me, though at first, I thought it was just his lunch coming back up... until I saw a sharp, dagger-like hook of the cave wall protruding through the thing's torso.

Damn, I knew lava tube tunnels could be jagged, but this was brutal.

I was apparently right about his lunch coming up, though, because after that came something sticky and black, in place of his blood. It began to ooze around the rock that impaled him, as well. Something was seriously wrong with these guys, and I wasn't going to take any chances with them.

I spun around to strike back at the one behind me when I saw Aphaera dive beneath me. She'd relinquished her bow, instead using her dagger. The narrow stream of the flashlight rolled toward the standing marauder just in time for Aphaera to see a weakness in his armor and slash toward the Marauder's ankle. She sliced through, sending him off balance as he roared out in rage, swiping around as the light turned away from us.

I joined in with her and attacked the enraged madman. I slashed with my machete, and he dodged it somehow, seemingly able to sense better in the dark than we could. But my persistence paid off, as the next slash caught him, and that sharp blade dug into his side. He screamed but tried to grasp my blade to yank it out.

I did him a favor and helped him, pulling it out of his side and his grasp, then repeating the strike again. Then, again. I hacked through his body with a wild fervor until I had severed his spinal column, and he was a twitching mess upon the black stone floor.

My chest heaved, I was splattered in so much blood and bile. But I'd won.

Though I hadn't banked on the monster impaled on the wall to rip himself free of the spike, the hole in his midsection knitting back together with inky black tendrils that crisscrossed over the wound.

Aphaera seemed to expect this, and she dodged forward, trying to repeat the motion of slashing his ankle. This one anticipated her move, though, and kicked her.

Hard.

She flew into the air and landed with a hard thud; the air stolen from her lungs. There was an awful silence that followed, and without her breathing, I couldn't even sense where she was anymore. The cave swallowed her sounds of life, even as it amplified the sickening *shlick* of flesh being sewn together by some unholy force.

I let loose a terrifying roar that was amplified by the cave, and then I charged, determined to repeat what I'd done to the other one to him. If he wouldn't die like a normal man, I'd hack him to bits so that the parts were too small to pose a threat to us.

But this one, despite being wounded, was tenacious, and fought with a frenzy of hatred and hunger. He gnashed his teeth as I slammed my arm into his chest and tried to slash at him. But he blocked the attack, and instead tried to rip into my forearm.

I wouldn't let him, but his claws dug into me and I gritted my teeth.

We were face to face, this monster and me. And I took him head on. I bashed my skull into his, which hurt since he had that damned metal face plate. But I heard his nose crunch beneath, and while he had some eldritch power to be mended back together, it still stunned him in the moment.

I would've struck with my blade again, but his grip on my sword arm was still tight. Instead, I pushed him back onto that spike, this time ripping a new hole.

Aphaera was like a specter, she moved so quickly and silently in that strange cave forged by thousands of years of lava. When I impaled him, she was ready, her smaller blade beginning to hack at his ankles as she seemed to understand my plan. He kicked at her again, but this time she was prepared, dodging the first kick and absorbing the weaker blow of the second. By the time he kicked a third time, his foot was held on by little more than the bone, and the momentum made her work all that much easier. There was the sickening sound of flesh rending, then beginning to slide without the tendons holding it in place.

It was the most harrowing battle I'd been through yet, but we saw it through. We persevered through the horrible goriness of it and hacked that Marauder to bits, until there was too little of him to knit back together.

And then, weary in both mind and body, I fell to my knees to catch my breath and pause a moment.

I had to fight off the gloom of the realization: if they all fought like this now, then we'd have little chance of victory. An army of them would be nigh unstoppable.

Aphaera stood, walked toward my flashlight, and gingerly picked it up. She inspected it before bringing it back to me. She was bruised, her blonde hair spackled with red and black blood, and she looked *tired*. As tired as I felt.

But she pushed on, going to our fallen comrade, and she began the unenviable task of collecting his possessions, just as the other tribesman had when we first encountered the ashki.

It was only a few moments before she stopped, her body poised like a cat as it neared its prey.

Her hands went to the lava stone beneath her, touching it and letting out a gasp that I saw more than heard.

I rose up and went to her, not wanting to let weakness overtake me for longer than that moment. I put a hand on her shoulder and asked, "What is it?"

"Power," she said, recoiling from it. "Awful, terrible power that should not be awoken."

She looked up at the cave ceiling and I guided my light there, showing the awful stalactites that descended toward us. The long, hollow tubes hung in thick clusters, and the blackish-silver glaze of the cave, mementos of the lava gases, looked like peeled paint. All around the edge of the cooled lava pool were driblet spires, still as gooey and thick as they were darker than night. Every few seconds, one of them dripped, causing a sizzle as it burned the rocks, and I pointed my flashlight around the cave floor.

Aphaera and I both realized at the same moment.

"This place lives. The volcano is trying to free whatever is trapped here. It would take time. But a sacrifice... they always hurry things along," she said, looking to our fallen ally. "We must not be here when it awakens."

I nodded to her words, feeling the same ghoulish fright that had entered me since we'd first seen that gory sight of cannibalism, and that unholy act of a creature being knit back together from death. Nothing about this cave system was right. It made the caves back on Earth I'd dared to explore seem like daycare by comparison.

"You're right," I said, "we should get moving."

But as my flashlight scanned the room, I saw many tunnels leading off from that round chamber, and none of them appeared the least bit more appealing than the last.

Aphaera scrambled off the lava rock, not wanting to be near its power any longer, not even bothering to finish her compassionate work of final rites for the tribesman. She had gathered a few things, and that would have to be enough. I watched her as she stilled in that cavernous maw, far from the boulder of power in the center. Her hand lifted, and she slowly guided it along before she stopped, pointing down one of the narrower, more jagged tubes.

"The air: it's warmer this way. More acidic. It will lead to the temple."

I stared in the direction she pointed, and while I could see nothing off about that tunnel compared to the rest... I got a chill down my spine. I felt something ominous.

But I nodded, then gathered my things and wits.

"Let's go, then. We have to stop them before it's too late," I said as I led the way.

But I'd be lying if I said I wasn't scared shitless by what we had just endured. And the most disturbing part? That wasn't the worst of what awaited us in those tunnels.

CHAPTER SIXTEEN

As we started down that tunnel, I could feel what Aphaera predicted: the flow of warm, acidic air. Eventually the all-encompassing darkness faded away, and I could put my flashlight back in my satchel.

There were red gemstones in the wall that seemed to glow like lava. And as we got in deeper, there were actual rivulets of that molten stone moving along, adding a glow to the tunnel. It was an aid to our vision, but also ominous. We were headed toward the heart of a fiery volcano that could turn rock into soup. I had to be insane.

We needed to be careful around it. The heat was so intense in the air, but it would be nothing compared to the touch of that lava. All it would take is one misstep, one stumble, and it could all be over.

The tubes meandered. That was the most natural part, how they wound in on themselves, created paths that didn't make sense. It was the only observation that helped remind me that this place wasn't made by man and it wasn't made for man. But as we squeezed through another cavern that was the perfect size for me, I marveled again at the fact that a cave could feel like home.

Even walking through this one on another world, in another realm of time and space, surrounded by unholy creatures and magic, when I felt the cave press in on me and give way, I was calm.

It was only when the tubes widened, and I felt exposed and surrounded by the cacophony of strange sounds, that chills went up my spine.

It was harder for Aphaera to guide us as we got closer to the source of the heat, the difference in air temperature much more subtle. She didn't talk much, not after encountering the stone of power, but her nerves seemed to have steadied a little as we got further from it.

We'd had to rest several times since then. Time didn't exist in the darkness of this place, and we had no idea how long we had before the ritual. We just knew that the only way to save Nyphenah was to persevere. We took turns on watch, and for the first time since we met, we didn't fill the days and nights with fucking.

There were no days and nights any longer. There was only a black pit of horror, and the brief reprieve of eerie red glow from the gems or the moving lava.

We had to have been in there for at least a day, but probably longer. We required stops to rest, eat, and sip what little water we had left in our skins to make it last. The air only got hotter the deeper we went, and that made me worry.

Would I end up dying down here? Not in a heroic battle, not to some slip or fall in a gutsy caving accident. But to thirst? I could already feel my body ripped down to just muscle and bone. Every bit of excess water had been taken from me, so that my muscles were bulging out hard and prominent with little fat to hide them.

But onward we went, regardless. I wasn't one who believed in turning back, after all.

And then, as we hit a larger chamber with branching tunnels, we confronted the enemy once more. Another Black

Marauder loomed in front of us and let loose a horrible banshee scream that no human should be able to make.

But instead of attacking us, he turned and ran. I began to pursue until Aphaera cried out a warning.

"It's a trap!" she screamed.

And with barely a moment to spare, I looked and saw it: the stones that were perched to fall from above. I skidded to a halt just in time to avoid being crushed in the avalanche of falling black rocks that sealed off the tunnel.

"Dammit!" I cursed, even though I should've been thanking Aphaera for saving my ass.

"We must be close," Aphaera said as the din of falling rocks quieted, leaving only ashy dust to choke out the air around us. It was harder to breathe with the oppressive, acidic heat bearing down on us. And without the source of fresh air coming through that tunnel, it was only going to get worse.

"Not anymore, we're not! What are the odds they didn't just seal off the tunnel leading to the temple, huh?" I growled, anger filling me.

"This close, all of the tunnels might lead us back to the temple; it's the source of the lava that made the tunnels after all," she reasoned.

I was still angry, refusing to give in and take some longer, circuitous route.

But then, as I gripped my blade's hilt, my eyes caught sight of an open tunnel above the one which collapsed. From it, some smoke filtered out, then up and up, through some more tunnels that must've led to the surface somewhere.

"Wait," I said, putting my machete away, then reaching for my climbing pick. "This tunnel up here… it probably joins onto the one they blocked off."

She looked where I pointed, and then she gave me a look, one I'd never seen on her face before. A look that said she thought I was mad.

"Malchor, you are mighty, but that ledge is too high and too smooth. It would be like jumping from sinking sand, only to grab onto glass, several feet above you."

But her words only made me smile.

"You mean like when we evaded the Demon in the Desert the first time?" I asked.

Sure, this wasn't quite the same thing. The distance was a lot higher, and the boulders were precarious. But we had the advantage of not fleeing from an unspeakable horror at that very moment, so I could think more clearly.

My remark did nothing to assuage her worries, but all the same, I prepared. I shed what was unnecessary and I fixed the leather wraps around my hands so I'd have a better, safer grip. I prepared for something that was exceedingly foolhardy.

"If you're coming, you're gonna want to climb on my back and hold on tight. Otherwise… I'll see you on the other side, over the corpses of our enemies," I said with such bravado, even an action movie star would've blanched.

She didn't like feeling afraid or weak. Mostly because she wasn't, but also because she had pride, and she wanted to please me. Whatever combination of those things rattled around in her mind at that moment, I saw her resolve waver.

"If I'm on your back, it'll increase your risk of failure," she said pragmatically, and I shook my head.

I let down my pick, walking toward her and cupping her face in my hand. She was dusty and bruised, her tanned skin not as golden as it was above ground, but she was still gorgeous. And she was still mine.

"Having you at my back will never increase my risk of failure," I said, my voice gentle and free of the ego that had built up in me since our journey began. I felt a little like my old self. Genuine, adventurous, and filled with passion. "You never have to worry about holding me back, Aphaera."

Her eyes twinkled with the tears and she blinked them

away. I leaned in, pressing my plush lips to hers, and even though my hardness throbbed between us, that's not what the kiss was about.

She made me realize, over and over, what life was all about.

"Then I will come with you, great Malchor, and I look forward to you surprising me once more."

I smiled at her warmly, having won her over. I kissed her again, then squeezed her hand.

"Then hold on tight. I don't want you to slip, or even jostle around. Cling with all your might," I said, as I turned from her and bent down to one knee to make it easier for her to climb onto my back.

She shifted her supplies so that they were in a more comfortable resting position, before her arms wrapped about my neck. Her soft breasts pressed against my back as her thighs tightened around my hips.

"I'm ready," she whispered in my ear.

I rose up with all the confidence I could muster, showing no sign of her added weight burdening me. And then I peered up again…

What was I thinking?

If I had a climbing instructor with me, he would've cursed me out and told me the trip is over for trying such a thing without a rope and harness. But I rarely ever lost my grip on a rock wall or cliffside. Rarely ever. But then, I'd also never tried it with another human on my back before either.

I decided not to think about it too much, and I began to climb over some of the rocks at the blocked entrance. Once I got to the top of them, it was just sheer, smooth rock wall. No more jagged knives, no more protrusions, no more leverage to grab onto. But that was good. The smoother the stone, the more recent the wear, the closer we were to the opening.

I took a moment to inspect it in the dim lighting, and made out some folds in the solidified magma. I reached up and grabbed on, then found another place to dig my climbing pick into. That trusty tool had saved my ass many times, and now it was doing so again as I heaved myself up and up.

I grunted and felt Aphaera's grasp on me tighten, as we reached a dangerous height. There were fewer potential points to grip onto at all. A fall at that point would've been devastating, though hopefully not fatal. But we would have to go higher still if we were going to make it out.

We continued up and up, until we neared that gaping crevice where the smoke poured out. I struggled to find another grip, something to hold onto. Until I saw it.

A sharp protrusion that would tear through my hand if I tried to grip it. I hoped the lizard-leather I had wrapped around my palm would do the trick as I reached out for it.

That sharp, coarse rock sliced through my leather and bit into my flesh, and I gritted my teeth as I put my and Aphaera's weight on it. We were oh so close, I wasn't about to give up.

I'd been in some tight spots before, and whenever I found myself in one, I told myself the same thing: *"Temporary pain. Long term gain."*

I repeated the mantra to myself then, ignoring the burning sensation as the rock dug further into my palm. I was using my off hand, not willing to injure my sword hand, but it would still put me at a disadvantage.

It's not like I had any other options.

I pressed on upward, digging my climbing pick into a new spot, and was able to release that cutting stalactite. And then, finally, I had my hand on the cusp of the entrance to that opening, and I pulled us both up.

But as I got there, the smoke clouded my vision and made us both cough. I couldn't see that the tunnel it poured out of was smooth and far too steep to rest on. So just as our bodies heaved up there… we slid down. Into the ashen unknown.

It was but a few seconds, but it felt like eternity as we slid down and down, through choking smoke. And then, we spilled out of the tunnel.

Only through gut instinct and reaction did I manage to throw up my climbing pick and cling to the edge of that tunnel which had betrayed us moments before, but now held us in place.

So I, with Aphaera clinging to my back, dangled from that opening on the other side. We loomed over a pool of lava below that bubbled and popped and hissed at us, as it produced that caustic smoke that burned our eyes and lungs.

She whimpered as she held onto me, her nails digging into my chest, but she didn't jostle or struggle, thankfully. Because if she had, we'd have been sent careening to our deaths. Her stillness gave me the time I needed to look around.

The lava was so bright, and after so long in the pitch black, it was almost searing to our eyes. I didn't have time to waste, though, and I scanned our surroundings.

After agonizing moments of blinking smoke and ash from my eyes, I saw the pathway the Marauder must've taken after dropping those stones to block the entrance. But it wasn't directly under us. It was a couple feet to my right.

"Aphaera," I said, "my sweet…"

I licked my lips. "Take my hand. I'll swing you over to the walkway to safety," I said, offering her my free hand, bloody from the cut I'd suffered.

She tightened around me, not wanting to let go. The poor woman was trembling, and I hated having to ask her to do such a thing, but it was the only way.

She had to trust me. Trust me with her life.

And slowly, her arms loosened from my neck, her hand wrapping around my wrist, letting my hand wrap around hers in turn. It provided us more strength, but we'd have to time the release perfectly.

I believed in us.

Her athletic body was in control as she lowered herself from my back, her weight slowly transferred to my one arm.

I make it sound so simple now, but when you're dangling from a rocky crevasse, being blasted with fiery heat and smoke, suspended from one arm holding a weathered pick… nothing is easy or clear. And definitely not safe.

It took me a while to muster my courage, to bravely try to swing my partner to that walkway without shaking my own precarious hold. But I began, in earnest, swaying her beneath me as I tried to get her onto that stone to safety.

I swear, time froze as we reached that perfect point and our two hands disentangled in perfect unison. I watched the most beautiful and perfect woman I'd ever seen fall through darkness toward molten rock… or salvation.

My heart skipped a beat when her first foot slipped on the edge of the walkway, but the second foot caught, and she scrambled on top of the stone. For a moment, I didn't care if I made it. I was just glad she did. I could've died happily then and there, knowing I gave her a chance.

And when the pick slipped just a bit, and I lost my grip on the rim… I felt like my time had come. But that wasn't my fate.

My pick caught at the very rim, on some rock that I knew wouldn't stay put long. There was no time for fancy maneuvers, to sway and try to topple myself toward the path. I had to just fucking do it, or else fall to my death in that instant.

So I went with it, and as the rock gave way, I swung the climbing pick toward the walkway. And with the pick and a bloody hand, I grabbed on, catching myself from tumbling into annihilation, with only the task of hauling my sweat-glistening body up onto it.

There was Aphaera's hand reaching out for mine, her heels dug into a crevice that would help her maintain her own footing. I thrust my arm toward her and she grabbed on with both hands. My muscles tensed and bulged, the heat and thirst making my head foggy, my motions less fluid.

I was far too heavy for her to lift by herself, and my left hand was injured, weakening my own ability to haul myself up. But, with her assistance and my raw muscle, we did it. I rose up, panting, my sweaty chest heaving as we lay there for a moment, catching our breath and celebrating our victory.

If we weren't in a volcanic cave of ash and flowing magma, I'd have taken her right there.

The way she looked at me, her pouty lips parted as she panted for breath, I knew she felt the same.

We smiled at each other, triumphant but restrained. We weren't at the end of our path yet, and more Marauders might be lurking nearby.

We stood on shaky legs, adjusting to the glorious feel of solid stone beneath us, when Aphaera caught something out of the corner of her eye. She swiveled and pointed, and I looked just in time to catch a glimpse of something. A flash of light. I didn't care if it was a sun or more of that horrible lightning, or even just a different type of glowing mushroom. It was white light, and I knew we were close.

I rose up and took out my blade, leading the way as we headed toward the exit. The sight we saw was nothing to be thankful for. Terrifying, grisly doom sat on the other side, and General Zarizh stood there at the center of it all, awaiting us.

CHAPTER SEVENTEEN

We were perched on the edge of a narrow, precarious path on the inside of the volcano. Smoke rose up, ash and fire seemed to fill the air, but there was light. At least there was that.

Part of me was surprised we made it in so little time, but the tunnels had provided a direct trail, whereas the tribal army was having to trek around the craggy hills and mountain sides. But then, I'd lost track of time anyhow. Maybe it was longer than I realized.

Regardless, at that moment I was transfixed: down in the center of the volcano, as if hewn by some unholy god or goddess, was a great platform suspended over the magma below. A hideous temple of black and red stone carved with the visages of ghoulish monsters.

There amid the columns stood the towering General Zarizh, and before him a sacrificial altar, upon which was strapped a nude maiden. It had to be Nyphenah, but I couldn't see clearly from such a distance.

I looked at Aphaera knowingly, for all that was left to do was descend that path to the heart of the temple.

We hadn't been spotted yet, and I wanted to use that to

our benefit as long as possible. Our steps, our every motion had to be slow enough to not draw the eye. We had to use the shadows and flashes of light that the volcano produced to our benefit. If we got close enough, perhaps Aphaera could cripple Zarizh with an arrow, but after what we saw in the caves, I didn't want to make any bets that he would be an easy foe.

But as we moved lower, closer to the scene of the arcane ritual, I did feel some comfort in the fact that I saw nobody there to help him. His Marauders must have all been stationed at the volcano entrance from the outside, awaiting the tribal army. That would be to my advantage, at least.

We went down and down, the pathway far longer than it appeared from above. But finally, we reached the bottom, where the path deviated toward the platform suspended in the center. I nodded to Aphaera as she readied her bow, knowing that it would be best for us both if she hung back with the advantage of height and distance, as I went in.

I opted for my spear, putting the machete back at my side. Some distance between Zarizh and I was needed. And caution. The spear was the right weapon for that.

I was so close, near enough to reach out and strike when Aphaera's arrow sailed through the air and found its target. Zarizh's armor was more elaborate than the Marauders', his helm practically a crown, and topped with spikes. The dark metal was eerily thick, yet supple, and there were so few weak spots.

But Aphaera found one.

At the perfect angle, at the perfect degree, at the perfect calculation of his breathing and motions and the thickness of the air, her aim was true, and pierced within the narrow slit that revealed Zarizh's eye.

A fierce cry filled the already-deafening volcano as his sharp, fang-like teeth gnashed the air in pain. I timed my attack to coincide with Aphaera's and pounced! I plunged my spear into the General, stabbing in deep until the steel tip came out the other side.

All around us, it was as if the volcano itself had been hurt. Great jets of molten magma rocketed up around the sides of the temple platform and plumes of black smoke billowed up. It was like we'd struck the death blow against the volcano and the General all at once!

But of course, nothing is ever that easy. At least, not when dealing with some dark magic prick like Zarizh.

His ruby red gaze turned on me as he ripped the arrow from his eye and his claw-grasp gauntleted hand reached out to grab me by my leather armor. He hauled me in closer, as I saw his other hand pull out his iron blade.

I resisted and pulled back, our two great mights in direct competition. But in the end, the loser was my armor, because it ripped away in his hand as I jerked back, leaving me bare and glistening from the waist up as I gripped the end of my spear.

But his blade just sliced through the handle as I tried to pry it free, leaving me with just the end. I dropped it and reached for my machete as he came at me. While Aphaera landed another arrow into him, it did nothing to hinder him, but only caused more jets of lava to spew up around us.

We were engaged in a melee, Zarizh and I. Despite his injuries, his motions were graceful, refined. He was a wraith in battle, moving with elegantly sweeping motions, his blade skillfully moving through the air and slashing at me with such expertise.

It was all I could do to avoid getting gutted by him as I finally freed my own machete and was able to deflect his attacks.

But I pressed on all the same, and an upward retaliatory strike sent my blade slashing across his face. His faceguard helmet had protected him from the worst of it, but my attack knocked it free.

I got to look upon his face at last.

Ignoring his sharp fangs and his deathly pale complexion, he was a man that might've been described as beautiful. With long, stark white hair, a striking face, and refined features, he would've caught the eye of most any woman. But he was the devil himself, as far as I was concerned. And we clashed with all we had.

He was a better sword fighter than I, and filled with some unholy power from the volcano around us. But I was spry and my weapon was better made. I did something I wouldn't have risked otherwise and struck at his sword directly with my own. The iron was cleaved in two, leaving him with but a hilt in his hand.

I grinned, feeling that, while he was my greatest foe yet, I was prepared for this. I was going to take him down at last. My engagement with his unholy disciples in the cavern below had taught me what to expect, and I was going to hack him to bits, just like his minions.

But as I was about to press my advantage, his broken sword lit up in flame! Where his iron blade once was, now a magical blade of pure fire took form, and he met my attack with a parry of his own. That fire licked at my blade and hands, as he deflected my attack so easily.

Aphaera couldn't strike him, not as we fought so close together, not as the lava still danced so high with every wound we inflicted upon him.

I was alone in my struggle, the beautiful Nyphenah bound to the altar and Aphaera unable to help.

It all came down to me. To be the man that my women believed me to be.

To be the man that I hoped I was destined to be.

Zarizh moved with grace and speed as his ruby red eye was knit back together in front of me. An arrow popped from his flesh as black tendrils extricated it and began to seal the wound. And while I pushed the attack continually, he just kept parrying and deflecting.

My opening advantage was fading away, as the wounds we'd struck healed, and he grinned at me, as if he knew it was just a matter of time before he was back to full strength. I could even see the end of my spear edging out of him until the steel tip clattered to the stone.

Out of the corner of my eye, I spotted Aphaera moving toward the altar. She was watching me, moving slowly as I'd shown her, but she was my woman. I was always going to see her. I understood her plan, and I knew my role in it.

I had to keep Zarizh from looking at her. I had to make him think he had an advantage on me, one believable enough to make him take the bait.

And what I came up with was to haul out my pick and dual wield it with my machete. I came at him with a great roar that even managed to compete with the roar of the volcano around us, as it spat fire and vomited black clouds of ash.

I attacked him with a frenzy, forcing him to be on guard. I put his skills with his fiery blade to the test, as he struggled to keep up with the blows coming from two weapons at once.

He moved about like a black ghost, but I kept him on the retreat, successfully distracting him from Aphaera and Nyphenah. But then... he caught sight of them, and the volcano roared with rage! Or maybe it was one, then the other. I'm not sure anymore. Perhaps it was whatever dark entity inhabited that volcano, the one who mended the General's skin with unholy magic, that had alerted him.

Regardless, he sprang into action and parried away my blows. Then, in a daring move that, looking back, I have to admire him for, he struck me. The fiery edge of his blade sliced across my chest and shoulder and left a burning, bleeding mark there. The stench of my own flesh sizzling struck my nostrils as I reeled.

And I saw the flame-wielding nightmare race toward my women. Everything seemed to slow down in that moment as I watched in horror, wounded and weary.

Aphaera saw it and dodged out in front of Nyphenah, protecting the prone woman. Her daggers were in hand, but the flaming sword would make her have to get in much too close to make use of them. It was all she had, though, and she was not going to go down without a fight.

She ran towards Zarizh, a scream coming from her mouth as she daringly put herself in the fray, dodging the first swing of his sword.

"You will die for what you've done," she cried out, her toned body glistening from the heat and glowing in the flames of the lava.

Zarizh laughed, a menacing, cruel sound that echoed around us. The volcano seemed to breathe, to expand, to laugh along with him.

"I will make you my own personal pet!" Zarizh taunted her as their blades clashed, an expert fighter facing my nimble, perfect Aphaera. "I will twist you into shape to become the Banshee Queen of my Marauders!" he rasped as they fought.

But his taunt had an unintended side effect. To hear another man talk about claiming my girl filled me with rage, and fueled my body as I lifted myself up and charged in. Such intense fury powered me that even when he detected my attack and pivoted to handle us both at once, I just threw my pick, letting it spin through the air for his face.

He grabbed it from the air in a display of battle prowess that startled me, but I was undaunted. And as he threw my own pick back at me, I didn't relent.

I tumbled forward in a roll, dodging the pick and coming up at him. My machete found his midsection, cleaving up through his flesh nearly a foot, and sent a scream of agony reverberating through the whole volcano. The rock walls shook as he and it wailed.

Aphaera joined in to help me finish him off and hack him to pieces, but even with my machete embedded in his torso, he had plenty of fight left in him. He used his clawed hands to attack her, knocking her daggers from her hands and sending her sprawling. But that only gave me even more power.

I roared and used all the power in my body to split him up the middle, in a gory, gruesome act that made the heavens weep chunks of magma. The world around us shook violently, the volcano below us spewing fountains of red-hot lava.

And even in victory, as I saw life bleed from General Zarizh's face, it felt like ruin. From out of his body, a spectral ghost emerged. Its undying visage was barely visible and yet impossible to ignore, as it looked at me with enough boiling rage and hatred to make any man tremble.

As his body slumped lifeless to the floor, too damaged even for his dark god to repair, his specter stared at me with malice… and a hint of a mocking grin.

And he had reason to grin, because the volcano was about to erupt.

CHAPTER EIGHTEEN

Where I came from, I never had a chance to go to a volcano. That was far off, bucket-list shit.

But I knew a thing or two about them.

Hell, I think anyone with two brain cells would know at least this about them: do not be literally inside them when they erupt.

This volcano wasn't like the ones we had back home, not really, because the altar we stood on was something holy. Unholy. Whatever. It was raised up in the middle, above the lava, but it was still inside the damned volcano, which we'd just pissed off something fierce.

Aphaera grabbed her daggers, working to cut Nyphenah free of the dais as molten lava began to spurt up around us. I ran for my pick, looking around the sides of the volcano and trying to find the best way for us to escape when I saw a small spurt of lava fall down in front of me. Another one landed further off, on the remains of my spear shaft, splintering it even as it lit on fire.

Shit.

I gathered my things as quickly as I could while I instructed the girls.

"We have to go **NOW!**" I shouted, and Aphaera was with me on that.

Nyphenah was wobbly from being off her feet for so long, but she knew that taking it easy was not an option. As I pointed to the path, my girls knew what to do, and we ran.

We pounded our feet against the hard stone as it began to heat up, knowing that it was now or never. The volcano and whatever powerful being inhabited it wanted its sacrifice, and if I wasn't willing to let Zarizh have one of my girls, I certainly wasn't going to let a volcano have one!

Nyphenah was not as athletic as Aphaera, but she knew what was at stake, and so she pushed herself hard, her heavy breasts bouncing against her ribs with each stride. It would have been super hot, if not for the fear that we were all going to die.

And who the hell knew what happened if someone died in the mouth of a volcano god?

We raced up another path, this one looking like it wound its way all the way to the top. I figured that was our best bet, as I led the way. The last place we wanted to be when this thing blew was inside its many underground tunnels, which the lava would flow through first.

The steps were hewn by man, it seemed. But long ago. They were now worn and battered, and the walkway narrower than I would've liked. Slipping and falling off the edge was a constant concern as the three of us made our way up and up the spiraling path.

But as we got about halfway up, I saw it, the last thing I cared to see: Black Marauders coming down for us, their black capes flowing behind them, swords in hand as they raced to stop us.

"We've got company," I shouted to my women.

I didn't know if they could hear me. The sounds of the volcano beginning to erupt were like dozens of grenades going off all at once, so I pointed with my pick, and Aphaera grabbed her bow. She let Nyphenah run ahead of her as she took aim, firing her shot at the front Marauder.

I was worried it wouldn't make it, the angle just slightly off, but then a gust of acidic smoke pummeled up, lifting it into position. It sailed through the air, and I guess it must have hit a spark somewhere along the way, because just before it hit her target, the arrow ignited into flame. It struck the Marauder's throat, flames spreading to his cloak, sending him off balance. His companions never even reached for him as he stumbled, careening into the magma below.

He landed hard on the thick liquid that was somewhere between stone and fire. It was several long seconds before the magma began to devour him, the process so agonizing and slow. It was not a good death.

I was not going to die like that.

So I steeled myself, readied my pick and machete, and charged at the oncoming Marauders. They were skilled fighters, and even with their boss dead, they still seemed to possess that unholy power. As I slashed one down the midsection, it began to heal before my eyes.

But one thing he wouldn't heal from any time soon was falling into the pit of lava below us, so I grabbed him as he reeled and threw him over the side. His unearthly screams reverberated and mingled with the chorus of booming artillery that was the volcanic eruption.

Onward I went, only to find more of the Marauders coming for us.

Even though I was able to take them on one at a time due to the narrowness of the stairs, they were slowing us down so much I felt like we were damned to die here; we'd never get to the top in time!

The wound across my chest stung, blood leaking from me, draining some of my precious strength as I went upward. Each time I had to swing my weapon it seemed to make the wound bleed a little more precious life fluid. And damn, did they make me have to work for each win.

I couldn't just mend myself by the will of some dark god, unlike those assholes.

Aphaera's arrows still flew, aiming toward the back so that she could thin out the numbers and avoid hitting me by accident. But the volcano seemed to realize her little ploy to use its own energy against it, and the air changed, seeming more chaotic. It sent more of my girl's shots flying wide, and every time she managed to land a strike, things changed again. It was keeping us on our toes.

Above us the crash of thunder boomed, as those balls of colored energy sparked between ash clouds. The air was quickly becoming unbreathable, and still the Marauders came.

I felt for a moment like Pyrrhus. I'd won the battle, but in doing so… I might have lost the war.

Because right then, the Marauder I faced dealt me another blow, adding a slash to my arm, taking it out of the fight. Things were looking grim for us all as the lava rose, swallowing the temple platform below and making its way up toward us. The Marauders seemed to have no fear of dying in that pit just to spite us, thanks to whatever unholy force drove them on.

The world seemed to go still for a moment as time slowed down. Everything seemed distant. And in that moment, I heard something: a soft, hissing, seductive voice that seemed to come from everywhere and nowhere, all around and yet from within.

"Stay, my precious. Stay and become one with me," it beckoned.

It was whatever dark force inhabited that volcano, trying to convince me.

Trying to make me stay and die in her fiery flames.

I'll admit now, long after the fact, that call was seductive and alluring. I was tempted for a moment to throw myself into the fire, that's how powerful it was. Or maybe it was just our bleak outlook helping her powers along.

I kept fighting, though, deflecting another attack, then thrusting back, getting him in the chest. Then he managed to rake his clawed grip over my shoulder, adding five more bleeding cuts to my flesh. Five more points from which my strength, energy, and will to live bled out.

I could become one with the flames, with the powerful volcano. I could swim through her caves, finding places never seen by mortal eyes before.

I paused, taking a step back, and the Marauder I was fighting didn't expect that. The momentum of his next blow was too powerful to meet only air, and instead it flung him off the side, into the volcano below.

But more still came. So many more, advancing down upon us.

Nyphenah was sobbing behind me, unable to fight. She had no weapons, no clothes. Aphaera was running low on arrows, and so few were hitting anymore.

All they had was me.

I shrugged off that moment of doubt, of fear, of desire to become one with something magnificent and terrible. If I was going to die, I was going to die fighting. I owed my girls that. I owed myself that. And I owed my allies that.

I became a terrible fury on that stone walkway. I hacked and slashed and did battle like never before, giving all I had left. And in that moment, when things seemed their bleakest…

The arrows rained down.

The 'cavalry' had finally arrived.

Nyphenah's tribe came over the ridge, and while the gusts of hot air and thick, fiery wind had swept Aphaera's arrows astray, the great rain of them the tribe brought was unavoidable. The Marauders began to fall like bulbs from a Christmas tree as you shook it hard. Their screams filled the smoky air as they plummeted to their doom far, far below.

Finally, we could advance at a greater speed, running once again. At least, as close to running as those precious, worn steps would allow. The remaining Marauders had turned back, facing the onslaught of the tribal warriors.

The lava was almost nipping at our heels, and I watched as one splatter rose high in the sky before crashing down on one of the Marauders. It splintered him in two, sending half his body one way, the other half another way, as if he'd been hit by an anvil in a Saturday morning kid's show... but with a lot more gore. Just one little splatter tore him in two.

We had to get the fuck out.

Some of the tribesmen went down, too, but I don't want to dwell on their ends except to say they were heroes, every last one of them. Brave warriors who persevered, even though they'd had no sign of me for days. They'd stormed the volcano to save Nyphenah without a lot of hope or awareness of the situation. And they'd saved us all.

When at last we crested out of that volcano, there was no time for celebration or relief. We just had to run, the whole lot of us. For while the magma rose at a slow pace, it spewed death at us and threatened to cut off our escape route. As we descended the long, winding trail down the black volcano, rivers of lava flowed all around, taking such strange and unpredictable paths. Several times we were nearly cut off, but still we persevered.

Only when we reached the relative safety of a nice, even slope did the weight of it all hit me: the loss of people, my own blood. And I passed out.

I don't know how long I was out for. I had dreams, though. Dreams of dark, cavernous maws, caves with jagged teeth that opened for me, consuming me. Dreams of power, of power beyond reality. Things that could not be, that didn't belong in my world or this one, but mine to command. An army spread out before me, chanting my name.

I woke once or twice, startled awake by something in a dream that was immediately out of reach. Corgash was beneath me at one point, carrying me, but I didn't remember much after that. The dreams were like an oasis, one I didn't want to leave.

But as I got farther from the volcano, they started to weaken their hold on me, their power softening as we left that horrid place in our wake. Yet even as it faded, I felt that imprint upon my very soul. I knew that the temptation of the volcano and the caves beneath would be a constant companion with me on my journey.

After returning to the tribe, I was treated like a hero. I barely remember those first days; I was so weary and wounded. The tribe traveled to their holy ritual place, an old temple built by people long, long ago. It was grand and beautiful, and there I was held as their champion, tended to by their best healers.

By Aphaera. And Nyphenah.

I awoke now and then to find them bathing me, cleaning and dressing my wounds. Until finally, I was well enough to proceed.

These people had no gods or spirits, no patrons to look over them. All they had was each other, and their temple reflected that. It was old, as old as the stones beneath it, and with such a history. Yet, newer finishes had been added: art of the tribespeople, of victorious hunts, landscapes they'd seen on their nomadic travels.

It was grounded in the mundane, but it was anything but. It was community, connection, appreciation for the natural gifts of the world and of each other.

The temple helped wash away the darkness that nipped at the back of my mind, trying to tempt me with unnatural power, and replaced it instead with earthly pleasures.

I looked around at the maidens, all working together to put up the flowers to fill the air with incense. Aphaera was at my side in a delicate white dress that clung to her curves, and she looked up at me with such love and affection.

Then there was Nyphenah. She stood at the front of the temple, her radiant smile lighting up the entire room.

Her dress was... unbelievable. It was a light fabric, nearly transparent, which one of the maidens explained to me was representative of how she would bare her soul to me, if only my hands were tender enough to peel back the layers without damaging the fabric.

She was decorated in jewels, gold chains around her arms, legs, and torso, to reflect the wealth that she would bring to me if I knew how to care for those precious metals and took the time to shine them.

Her hair was tied back, the fiery curls spilling about her face in a gorgeous halo, and her pale eyes found me.

It was the day we were to be bound together. The day she truly became mine.

I was still healing and in some pain, but seeing her like that, with Aphaera by my side, I felt whole once more. I got up from my recovery bed weary that day, but seeing her invigorated me.

It probably helped that I hadn't fucked in who knows how long. Longer than I had gone since I first met Aphaera, by far. Since we'd set off on our journey to rescue Nyphenah, we'd had no time to rut and enjoy the pleasures of our bodies. And then as I was recuperating, I was too worn down for it.

But seeing her then, I felt my cock stir, knowing that I'd get to experience that sweet girl's pleasures to my heart's content so very soon.

The ceremony, as had been explained to me earlier that morning by the chieftain, was a private one. It would be just the two of us, Nyphenah and I, and what happened was to be shared only between us.

I wasn't going to leave my Chief Consort out in the cold, however, and Nyphenah had helped convince her father. The three of us were going to be united, so it was only fitting that the three of us be present for it. It seemed like that had happened a time or two in the past, so even though the chieftain wasn't thrilled, well, he couldn't complain.

The respect he had for me in the aftermath of my heroics was firmer than steel, and our bonds would forever be united.

The maidens finished their decorating and shuffled out until finally, it was just the three of us.

I was garbed in those 'purifying' vestments now, the thin fabric billowy around me and doing little to keep me covered. My chest was bare, and I'd been adorned with some piercings in the recent days as I recovered. A tattoo was etched on my arms to mark my victory, to grant me strength in the time ahead, to protect my new woman. It all felt a little silly, but I didn't care, I went with it, humored their traditions and gifts.

Because what really mattered was this moment, the three of us in that sacred chamber as I approached young Nyphenah.

I reached out to cup her smooth face, to caress her cheek with my thumb as I looked down at her.

"I am so pleased we got to you in time," I said, my voice rougher and rawer since returning from the volcano. All that ash seemed to have given me a growly edge, but I was all smiles in that moment.

Aphaera hung back a little, letting me have some more personal time with my new girl.

Nyphenah turned her face, kissing my palm.

"I knew you would come for me," she said gently, her pale eyes flicking up toward me. Her skin was so warm to the touch, and so very soft. It was even better than in that dream that the mind beast had conjured in me, and this time, it was the real deal.

"So, what are we supposed to do for the ceremony?" I

asked, because that part was fuzzy. The chieftain just kept saying that it was individual, and there was no set ceremony for this sort of thing, but that was hard to believe. Back in my world, this type of event was the most scripted scenario a person could imagine.

"We swear ourselves to each other. Pledge to care for one another, and pick each other up when the other stumbles. But we did that in the volcano," she said with a soft, tender smile. "So all that's left is to celebrate each other's physical forms."

My smile grew at that, and I let my hand wander. I didn't dally, I didn't toy around, I just cupped her breast through that thin, gauzy fabric and let my thumb tease around her nipples, which I felt so prominently.

"You're a vision of beauty," I said to her in my growling voice.

I admired her as my dick stood up so stiffly it made my kilt into something obscene. But I looked back to Aphaera and said, "Undress her for me," before smiling at Nyphenah. "You're with us now. Forever more," I said, leaning in to press my lips to hers, kissing her slowly, passionately, deeply.

Nyphenah tasted like cinnamon and sugar, her soft body pressing into me. She was so feminine, her curves next to divinity, and knowing that she was a virgin? She was the perfect vision of youth and womanly appeal. It was to be my first time bedding a virgin, and I was excited to find out what it was like.

Aphaera approached us, her motions almost reverential as she went behind Nyphenah to untie the strings at the nape of her neck. The diaphanous straps of her top slowly began to descend, before fluttering to land atop her large, supple breasts.

I felt like a king already as I watched Nyphenah's unveiling, and while I wanted to reach out, to pull down that top and see what I craved, it felt more powerful to just stand and watch. To let Aphaera do the work of revealing my new concubine to me.

"I went into that volcano a man," I said to her, not sure where the words came from. Perhaps from the way she spoke of our 'union' or 'marriage,' or whatever you want to call it, being sanctified in the fiery pit of the earth. "But I came out feeling like a true King. Born of trial and flame," I said.

Nyphenah smiled brighter at my words, the warmth of it radiant as she nodded in agreement.

"You are my champion," Nyphenah said as Aphaera's nimble fingers gathered more of the fabric, letting it fall from Nyphenah's tits.

I'd almost forgotten how large they were, how perky and full, topped with stiff nipples that begged for my touch as Aphaera's hands found them instead. She touched my woman, grazed her fingers over Nyphenah's breasts before lifting one in her hand, offering it to me.

I took it, letting my strong fingers glide along Aphaera's dainty digits, then sink into soft yet supple breast flesh, squeezing and fondling her.

"You will bear many children for your new King," I told her, "serving me above all others."

I caressed her cheek with my other hand and smiled down at her, letting my eyes wander across her face and body. I soaked it all in as my dick throbbed and ached with desire to do more than just look.

"You will be second only to my first, who will guide and teach you on our journey together," I said, my eyes flitting to Aphaera with a glint of adoration.

Aphaera smiled back at me, so much love in her gaze. I knew she had to be pent up too, considering she hadn't fucked in a long time either. She had cum on my cock before we entered the volcano, on the night I decided that building my need for release would spur me on the journey ahead. But still, it must have been a challenge for her to put her own needs aside. She relinquished Nyphenah's breast to my hand and began undoing the strings and chains that held up the virgin's skirt.

There I was in front of that stunning, busty virgin that was mine for the taking, and my cock throbbed at the memory of how I restrained myself the last time with Aphaera. How I'd brought her to body-shuddering, screaming climax, but denied myself. It was a big contrast to the egotistical rutting I did before that.

But I enjoyed both. And as I toyed with Nyphenah's breast, I leaned in and kissed her again, my hands moving down to caress her sides. Then I confessed to my new concubine in a hushed murmur, "I have saved my seed for oh so long… and I ache to give it to you." The words rolled off my tongue growling and full of desire.

It felt like it was meant to be. Fiadh, the young maiden, had run off with my seed on the night our ceremony was to happen the first time. I'd gotten cocky, figured it was a good chance to see if Aphaera was telling the truth about my powerful virility. But now, in the special hall, as Nyphenah offered herself up to me, I was more potent than ever and in desperate need of a release. I was ready to fill her up, and my cock was becoming very distracting as it stole more and more blood from my brain as it stiffened.

The last of Nyphenah's robes were peeled away by Aphaera, leaving her in only those golden jewels that glittered around the glass above us. Her soft, feminine curves caught the light, and she was so beautiful. I'd seen her body before in the darkness of that yurt, but in the soft, warm glow, she was radiant.

She was so stunning, and even as pent-up and ravenous as I was, I still had to give her body a moment's appreciation. And in that space, Aphaera slipped around me, not needing the command to know to undress me now, though I had very little to shed. Wearing only a half-kilt, she undid the belt, then peeled it away.

I swear, I felt so fiery hot and ready to go--and the temperature was already so high--that I half-expected steam to rise up from my manhood as it lifted free. My shaft and balls swung so big and heavy, smoldering with desire. I gave a sigh at my new freedom and kissed Nyphenah before pulling back.

"I need to be inside you," I growled as I grasped Nyphenah by the hips and waist, then lifted her up, placing her ass upon the stone altar at the heart of our chamber.

Her legs spread readily for me, her sticky sweetness clinging to her inner thighs as they parted.

"I've been ready for you since that first night," she said, leaning in to whisper in my ear. "I've dreamt of this moment for so long. It was the only thing that gave me hope when I was tied to that altar. The thought of you coming and claiming me, then and there. I'm only sorry that the others got in the way."

Aphaera was at my side, watching, trying to anticipate my needs, but in that moment, I just wanted to bury myself in Nyphenah's wet, willing, virginal pussy.

But I had to restrain myself, if only for the sake of Nyphenah, who had never had a man inside her. I didn't want to seriously hurt her. And for Aphaera's sake, of course, since this was the culmination of her own cunning as much as my muscle and bravery.

So put my hands on Nyphenah's knees, parting them even further as I gazed down at that glistening pink slit, my own cock hovering near it, throbbing incessantly.

"My Chief Consort," I said, recalling the title that Aphaera had given herself. "Take hold of my manhood, guide it to the waiting maidenhood," I commanded.

In the past, I might have laughed at how formal it all sounded in my gruff tone, as two women offered themselves to me. But in that moment, it felt fated, like it was meant to be, and as Aphaera's soft hand wrapped around my thick, throbbing shaft, she smiled at me.

"As you wish," she purred, her gaze returning to Nyphenah as she brought my shaft to the other woman, until finally the crown of my shaft was gliding along her wet lips.

It would've felt wrong to exclude Aphaera from it all. And I wanted to be sure that Nyphenah appreciated the other woman's place in my heart.

Plus, it was fucking hot as hell to watch that dainty hand, grasping my thick, throbbing cock. Maybe I was just imagining things, but after so long without it, my dick felt bigger, heavier, hotter. It was pulsating and ready to unleash. As Aphaera rubbed that sensitive, purple tip against the young virginal slit, I shuddered and spurted pre-cum onto her.

I bent Nyphenah's legs back, until her knees were near her huge tits, and I let my enormous cock begin to push in against those slick folds, stretching them around my shaft as I claimed my prize.

Nyphenah held herself up with her arms so that she could watch, to see me take her, and that was even hotter. The three of us stared as Aphaera's hand guided me to those budding lips, letting me press into that tight, wet pussy.

I'd never fucked a virgin, didn't really know what to expect, but I did know that this would be one of the most memorable moments of my life.

As my crown finally pushed past her barrier and I heard her cry out, I felt triumphant. I still had so many inches left, and I wanted her to take all of it. All of me. But I was going to take my time, and make my girls savor it.

I moaned, feeling the head of my cock wrapped up in such a tight, untouched pussy. I greedily began to push deeper into her before I waited to ensure she was able to handle it. It'd been weeks since I'd last gotten off, and I was a beast of a man, my needs overruling my head as I grunted and pushed more of my dick into her.

"You'll bear the fruit of my loins on your first time," I rumbled, as I grasped her ankles and kept her knees back into her tits.

She was such a pale, untouched beauty, her full body folding for me as I took her. Even though it was her first time, she never seemed to be in an undue amount of pain. She moaned and whimpered, but that wet pussy was pleading for more, and Aphaera helped guide me in, encouraging me to take my prize.

"Yes, she will," Aphaera purred as her other hand trailed up Nyphenah's hips, her fingers playing along her skin.

I was done with taking it slow, trying to make our own little ritual. I just gripped Nyphenah's ankles, and began to powerfully rock my body, pistoning my cock into her tight little pussy. That slick canal slowly stretched open, strained to its utmost capacity as I dug in a bit deeper with each new thrust.

And all the while I ravenously watched her tits jiggle and sway from the force of my rutting.

I wasn't able to look at Aphaera, but when I spoke, she knew it was to her.

"Suck on her tit," I commanded.

Her fingers left Nyphenah's hips, and instead clasped that bouncing flesh, holding it steady as her mouth descended upon it. Nyphenah moaned as Aphaera's tongue lashed against her nipple, and it made her pussy even wetter, letting me spread her open even wider on my thick, throbbing dick.

If I'd been an ordinary man, the man I was before I stepped through that portal, I would have long ago blown my load. Well, I'd have never been in this situation to begin with, but if I had, I'd have been done for by then.

But the magic that Aphaera had unleashed upon me in the temple made me something more than a man. I was controlled, able to appreciate the way my dick tingled and throbbed as Nyphenah's pussy squeezed me so damned tight. It was beyond ecstasy, beyond anything. It was intensity on top of intensity, a feast for every one of my senses.

Instead, I was in full control, and it was like the sensation of cumming hard after a long build up, but it just kept going. I muscled through, pushing down the shivers as I held back my actual climax, drawing the moment out, ravaging my new former-virgin. I grew rougher, faster, harder. I pounded into her as I watched Aphaera suckle that perfect, fat, jiggling breast.

I moaned out loud, spurting more pre into my new concubine. My heavy, cum-laden balls slapped against her ass as I pounded and rutted away. That tingling need to unload was so powerful in me, but I resisted and kept resisting.

"This is the only cock you'll ever know," I growled out. "The only cock you'll ever touch, feel or taste. You belong to it now," I said, letting my perversions overtake me.

And it wasn't just hubris. Aphaera had said as much, showed me the magic that turned women into my willing slaves, and Nyphenah was already losing that battle. Her eyes were rolled back in her head, no longer able to watch me defile her. Nyphenah's screams, cries, and moans all combined into a perfect cacophony of pleasure as her tit was sucked and her pussy was fucked. All attention was on her for that moment, and every bit of precum I felt enter her weakened her mind to me more.

Nyphenah had seemed delicate to me from the moment I first saw her peeping on Aphaera and I in the yurt, but then and there, she was becoming mine. Bound to me, forever.

Now I had two women at my beck and call, serving me faithfully. That thought made my dick swell and throb even more, and I hammered into my new little virgin with the intent of making her scream and cum on my cock.

I looked down over my bulging pecs and rippling abs, and

watched the sight of my dick forcing itself into her up to the hilt. Our bodies struck together with loud, wet, lewd slaps that filled the chamber. I grunted and groaned, shuddering as I worked to make this girl scream my name and her allegiance.

"Who do you belong to?!" I growled at her as I bucked and thrusted, breaking in her virginal body in the most ravenously depraved way I could think of at the time.

"Malchor!" Nyphenah readily cried, trembling at the intensity of her own pleasure as I took her. Aphaera purred affectionately at the woman's breast, gathering her nipple between her teeth and tugging it, making Nyphenah cry out again.

"It's so good," she moaned, her body writhing.

Aphaera's other hand left my cock, letting me drive those last few inches into Nyphenah so deeply that I thought I might split her in two. Aphaera's fingers moved to Nyphenah's clit, though, and in that perfect, hedonistic moment, Nyphenah came. Her hot, wet fluids felt scalding as they bathed my cock and balls and Aphaera's hand, before flooding to the floor in a puddle beneath us.

I grinned and let my eyes roll back in my head as I reveled in the power and glory of having them both at once, of feeling the tight clench of a virgin pussy squeezing my dick to drain it dry. I moaned and bucked, my balls tightening as they prepared to unleash.

In that moment I forced my eyes open again to watch Aphaera tease the other woman's slit and breast. I released one of Nyphenah's legs to let it press against my chest, as I took hold of Aphaera by the back of her head and neck and drew her in to kiss her deeply. And there, over the glistening, shuddering body of my concubine, I made out with my sweet girl as I prepared to release my load.

As I drew Aphaera in, no longer at my side but pressed fully against me, it dawned on me.

That white dress had been unusual on her, but I figured it was for the ceremony. I had no way of realizing that it held a secret. But as her fuller breasts pressed against me, I felt a bump, lower down. It was still small, but firm and noticeable.

Even more so when she gasped against me, her mouth on mine.

"I wanted to show you once you were done. I didn't want your special day to be about us," she whispered. But once I knew, there was no going back. All the things she'd teased me about, telling me of my virility, about how she was bearing my son, I half disbelieved. But feeling that baby bump press into my hip, there was no longer any doubt.

I was going to be a father. In that moment I was ravenous with joy, exulting in the thrill of it.

For so long it had felt like an illusion, a lovely thought, but I didn't fully buy it. But now I was full of joy.

"Everything is about us from here on out," I growled into Aphaera's ear, as my dick throbbed and spurted inside another woman.

I kissed Aphaera deeply, passionately, even as my pace grew more erratic, until finally…

Our lips parted as I gasped and moaned, and my cock began to erupt. Thick strands of my virile seed flooded into that young virgin womb, as I groaned and shuddered in the absolute bliss of my long-overdue release.

Aphaera was pressed to my side, massaging my skin as she watched me fill another woman. There was no jealousy, no fear, just desire and respect radiating from my Chief Consort.

Nyphenah cried out, her pussy tightening around me in response to my orgasm. She was cumming again, her muscles milking me of my seed and pulling it deeper and deeper as her body opened for me like a flower.

There was something radiant in that moment, and maybe it was all bullshit I told myself, but I swear, I felt our connection in a primal way. I felt my seed make contact and it was the most intense sensation.

If all Aphaera said was true--and I no longer doubted any of it--my mighty, hard cock was laying claim to Nyphenah in a way that was hard to parallel in the real world. I not only claimed her virginity, I was sowing my seed in her womb, making her bear my child. And more than that, my seed was marking her, mind, body, and soul, as mine. Creating an addiction within her for me that would never end.

I roared out my satisfaction as I claimed her, clutching Aphaera to me in one arm, gripping Nyphenah's breast in another, and letting that tight pussy drain me of every last drop I had to give.

The intensity of that moment did not dim for some time, and the passion that built between the three of us was intoxicating in its own right. My seed might twist women to my whims, making them my willing slaves, but the magic I possessed would pale in comparison to the magic that we could create.

Together.

ABOUT THE AUTHOR

R.A. Masters is an erotic writing duo! He creates the vision, she creates the sexy art, and together we take our creations on an adventure through exotic fantasy lands where the man gets to prove himself in a harsh new world, and win all the women.

These stories are dripping with alluring girls, and led by a powerful man, just the way we like it. And we adore every opportunity to explore the dynamics of their harem relations in… intimate detail.

Born in the country, they love exploring the wilderness, old abandoned sites, and the occult. Not to mention the deviously sexual. All the fascinating areas of the world that civilized people shy away from.

Sign up for their Newsletter to be updated of all their hot new releases: http://smarturl.it/RAMastersNewsletter

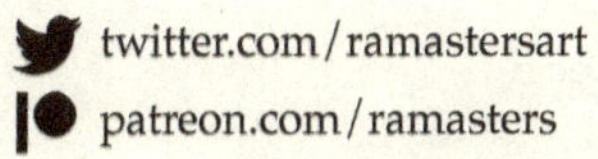

twitter.com/ramastersart

patreon.com/ramasters